MW01078926

Sounds Like LOVE

LAURA FORD

FriesenPress

Suite 300 - 990 Fort St
Victoria, BC, V8V 3K2
Canada

www.friesenpress.com

Copyright © 2021 by Laura Ford
First Edition — 2021

Illustrations Copyright Fiona Kerridge 2020

All rights reserved.

No part of this publication may be reproduced in any form, or by any means, electronic or mechanical, including photocopying, recording, or any information browsing, storage, or retrieval system, without permission in writing from FriesenPress.

ISBN
978-1-5255-9299-7 (Hardcover)
978-1-5255-9298-0 (Paperback)
978-1-5255-9300-0 (eBook)

1. YOUNG ADULT FICTION, ROMANCE, CLEAN & WHOLESOME

Distributed to the trade by The Ingram Book Company

TABLE OF CONTENTS

For Nanny,
your love and appreciation for cats
and all animals continues in us all.

For Lille,
the cat who inspired so much of this book.

CHAPTER 1

A Surprise

It was springtime in the quiet village of Sunnymede and change was in the air. The fields were lined with daffodils dancing in the breeze, nodding their heads as if knowing an unspoken secret. Wendy didn't know it, but today there was a very unexpected surprise waiting for her as she visited her grandma's house for the last time. Change was coming for her, whether she liked it or not.

Wendy stood alone in the living room of her grandmother's old red brick cottage, her auburn hair fell loosely at her shoulders, contrasting against her green coat, and a large wicker cat basket sat beside her. Inside the basket, a tabby cat with black and brown markings and big green eyes looked out at her timidly.

Now that her grandma had passed away, Wendy's parents had sold the cottage to some people who were new to the area. Wendy had come to collect a box of keepsakes which had been left for her – special things that had belonged to Grandma that she wanted Wendy to have. These mementos, she would remember her grandma by.

Today, however, it seemed that not only was Grandma's house rapidly being cleared of all her possessions, but Grandma's tabby cat had been left alone in a basket for Wendy to collect as well – without even so much as a note!

Wendy was dumbfounded. Looking down at the cat in the basket, she shook her head. Wendy couldn't believe that her parents would do this; she really couldn't stand cats!

The little cat poked her pink nose out from between the wicker slats and sniffed up at Wendy, her delicate nostrils twitching, and Wendy looked down at her, remembering her childhood. She thought back, remembering all of her parents' pedigree show cats – they took up every waking moment. She sighed, realising that her parents wouldn't want just an "ordinary" cat like this one.

Wendy felt overwhelmed at the prospect of having to care for the unwanted cat. Even though she was young, just nineteen, Wendy had recently received some very challenging news. Wendy had begun to lose her hearing and this was making her life much more complex. Recently, doctors had told her it was possible that, over time, she would lose her hearing completely. In the meantime, there would be a gradual weakening, more and more over time. It was a lot to come to terms with and there was no way that she wanted to take on a cat to add to the pressure she was already feeling. She tapped her foot next to the cat's basket, worrying about how she was going to handle the situation.

Inside the basket the cat watched Wendy's tapping foot, and her pink nose quivered as she sniffed the air. Strange smells of men and boots and mud filled her little nostrils, and she gazed out with her green Cleopatra eyes.

The poor little cat didn't know what was going on or why her home was changing around her. All of the furniture was being taken away and her home was being emptied. The cat watched with confusion as her favourite red chair disappeared from view and out the front door.

Upstairs in the cottage, there had been a wooden chest of drawers beside the bedroom window; from here the cat would sit and keep watch over the gravel driveway down below. She liked this spot because she could see clearly who was coming to the front door and could then promptly let Wendy's grandma know. But today the bedroom furniture had been the first to vanish.

Now, nearly everything in the cottage was gone, and unfamiliar sounds echoed around the bare rooms like a small cave.

Two surly removal men wearing brown overalls carried a varnished wooden table down a narrow corridor to the front door, their boots squeaking on the wooden floor.

The men continued out through the open door to their large grey truck – they had been removing boxes, furniture, and different things from the cottage all morning.

Now, as Wendy looked down at the cat basket again, a cool wind snaked its way down the hallway and into the small wooden-beamed living room where she stood, making her shudder. It was Spring, but there was still a chill in the air. She wrapped her green coat tightly around her.

Suddenly, a brazen gust of wind billowed through the front door, slamming it effortlessly with a loud bang. The door latch snapped shut, as if barring the wind from entering again, and the glass in the doorframe shook with the force of it all.

Wendy jumped at the loud intrusion on her quiet thoughts, hunching her shoulders in shock. She looked around the living room with her big blue eyes – it was now almost empty of any furniture.

Wendy had so many good memories in Grandma's home. It was sad for her to see it empty when she remembered how Grandma had made it so beautiful. The walls were decorated with beautiful, honey-golden wallpaper with white velvet flowers impressed upon the surface. Wendy remembered the day Grandma had redecorated the living room this way, how she had smiled when it was finished. Grandma's home had always been full of art and flowers and the wonderful aromas of her cooking.

Why did you have to leave me now? Wendy thought. Grandma had understood exactly what Wendy was going through when it came to losing her hearing; Grandma had lost her own hearing in her later years and was a master at lip reading and sign language. She made everything look so easy and had always encouraged Wendy. Now, there was no one who understood what she was going through.

Grandma had always been there for Wendy, which helped to make up for the fact that her parents were always busy with their one hobby – their one and *only* hobby, or you could call it an obsession – taking their pedigree cats to compete in cat shows all over the country and, sometimes, the world.

This meant that they often left Wendy on her own as a child and, as a result, Grandma became like a second mother to her. With Grandma, Wendy wasn't second best to any silly posh cats.

Wendy moved to face the French doors which opened out onto Grandma's small, neat back garden; she knew it so well. She looked through the doors at a blackbird hopping across the round green lawn in search of worms.

Pink hollyhock flowers – one of Grandma's favourites – swayed in the breeze. They had planted them together the previous spring. It felt like two seconds ago that they were together. A small cherry tree blossomed, its frozen pink petals slowly drifting down to the lawn on the breeze.

The garden was a beautiful little space and, despite its size, Grandma had made it a welcome home for many creatures. There was even a gnome – he sat beside a small oval pond, smiling broadly, holding a fishing rod in his sturdy hands.

The gnome wore a bright royal blue jacket and a pointed hat which was a cheerful cherry red; his cheeks were equally as red, like fat strawberries. He was about thirty years old but he didn't look it – thanks to Grandma's meticulous care. Wendy remembered Grandma liked to touch up his paint now and then to keep him respectable.

"What would the neighbours say?" Grandma used to joke when he got a little bit dirty. "We can't let them see you like this!"

Wendy smiled, remembering fondly.

"Mr Nettles," she said out loud to herself, remembering. Yes, his name was *Mr Nettles,* the gnome – the *Gnome of Sunnymede.*

Wendy's attention was taken from the garden and her memories by quiet creaking sounds coming from the wicker cat basket. The cat was moving inside to get more comfortable, re-settling herself in a little oval.

Wendy turned her eyes back to Mr Nettles and her memories. She was lost in her thoughts when, as if by magic, a yellow butterfly appeared in the air near Mr Nettles. It drifted on the wind, floating in the air around Mr Nettles, its movements scattered like the blossom petals. It flitted this way and that until, finally, it landed on his shining blue shoulder.

It opened and closed its delicate sunshine-yellow wings and warmed itself in the gentle sunlight, which hazily made its way through the tufted clouds above. Wendy smiled at Mr Nettles – he was a ray of sunshine on a very sad day.

As Wendy watched the butterfly, she felt a breeze of cool air against her shins. She turned from the window and looked at the door beside her. At the bottom of the door, a small cat flap moved gently in the breeze. It had been carefully cut into the wooden door-frame many years ago, and it led directly to the garden.

Wendy sighed heavily and knelt down beside the cat flap. She moved the little brass latch across it and closed it permanently – the end of an era.

CHAPTER 2

The Cat Fanciers

Wendy was fired up and ready to ask her parents why they had abandoned Grandma's cat. What was she supposed to do with it? With a scowl, Wendy pulled her phone from her pocket and was about to press her parents' number. At that moment, one of the removal men who had been clearing Grandma's house strode up to Wendy with a brown box full of different items. With a forced smile, the man thrust the box at Wendy. A large vase protruded prominently from inside the box, wobbling with the sudden movement.

Surprised, Wendy took the box and peered into it. It was heavy and full of keepsakes from Grandma's house.

"Thanks," she said, steadying the wobbling vase as the removal man marched out of the room. She smiled sadly and returned to her phone, hitting 'dial' on the screen. As the phone began to ring, the removal man now appeared in the room again, this time with a small white envelope in his hand – he waved it at her, smiling.

"I forgot this," he said, poking the envelope towards Wendy.

"Derek, where have you wandered off to?" the other removal man yelled gruffly from upstairs. When the downstairs removal man heard the voice, his eyes widened. Wendy's hands were full; she had the brown box in one hand and her phone in the other, so she quickly tilted the box towards the removal man so that he could drop the envelope in.

Hastily, he dropped the envelope into the box and thudded across the room towards the hallway, calling out, "I'm coming, I just had to give the young lady that box from upstairs!"

In his haste, however, the envelope didn't quite make it into the box. Instead, it tumbled into the wide brim of the vase, fluttering down inside and disappearing from anyone's view.

Wendy didn't notice the envelope's disappearing act; she was more concerned with her phone call. These days, phone calls were beginning to cause her anxiety. She turned up the volume on her phone as it rang.

Each time Wendy used the phone, she was reminded of the major changes she was facing in her life. She had a demanding life – creating websites, designing all kinds of webpages, logos, and even blog posts – and she loved it.

She was taking classes for lip reading and sign language to prepare for the future and this took up a lot of her time. On top of everything, she had home study as well. Making sure that she was a proficient signer meant everything to Wendy. She wanted to make sure that she could talk with her hands the same way that she could with her voice.

All of these things went through her mind as the phone rang. Wendy needed her parents to take responsibility for the cat – and besides, they were the ones who were the cat lovers. *Everything* in their lives was all about their "perfect" show cats.

The phone seemed to ring for a long time. Finally, her father answered. He sounded out of breath; he must have run to the phone.

"Hello, Wendy!" he called into the phone, a smile on his face.

He stood in the kitchen of his home wearing an apron with a large, round cat's face on it. He had been cooking breakfast and held a wooden spoon in one hand.

"Hi, Dad," Wendy said, an urgency rising in her voice. "Thanks for the box. Listen I need your help, I –"

"Oh, glad you got it, dear!" Dad interrupted breezily. "Grandma wanted you to have those things. Is everything OK?"

"Well," Wendy began, trying to think of a way to phrase her surprise at the appearance of the cat in Grandma's house. "What is going on? The cat is back here at Grandma's – sitting in a basket." She raised one hand to her forehead in exasperation as she spoke. "Why is she back here? I thought that she was living with you now."

"Oh right, dear," Dad replied, scratching his head with the handle of the wooden spoon. "Well, I don't know how we can help you, really. That was just *temporary*."

"Temporary?" Wendy raised her eyebrows. "What do you mean, *temporary*?" She began to pace about the room. "Dad, you know I don't like cats, I can't take care of one – I've got too much –"

"Well, take it to the local shelter then, dear. Mum is just too upset to think about anything right now. We knew the day would come – Grandma was not doing well – but it still came as a shock that she's gone." He lowered his tone. "Your mother is *not* having a good day. She's been crying about Grandma all morning." He looked back towards the living room where Wendy's mother sat, sunken into the sofa, sniffing and loudly blowing her nose into a tissue.

"I know, I loved Grandma too, Dad," Wendy said sadly. "She was always there for me."

"Yes, of course, we all loved her very much – she was one of a kind," Dad said sadly, holding back his emotions.

Wendy felt frustrated – everything felt like a mess. She didn't like cats and she didn't want to face being reminded of Grandma and how much it hurt losing her. Seeing Grandma's cat every day would just make her feel sad.

"She would have wanted *you* to have the cat, Dad," Wendy said, feeling her cheeks getting hot. "You're the ones who are the cat people."

Wendy's dad sighed. "You know we can't take the cat, Wendy; we have Martha and Kiki to think about."

Martha and Kiki were Wendy's parents' prize-winning show cats. They were very fluffy and very posh. They had won many awards and ate only the finest fish. They were pure show cats – very picky and very pampered.

Wendy's mother sat there on the sofa, still holding her handkerchief. She had big fluffy hair, just like the show cats, and wore a bright pink top with black leggings that were patterned with white cat-paw prints.

The living room where she sat was filled with trophies and rosettes from all of the cat shows at which their previous show cats had won prizes, and now Martha and Kiki were adding to the haul of trophies. Martha and Kiki were on the front of several of the cat magazines. They were so well known that they even had commercial sponsorships from companies who paid to have Martha and Kiki posed with their cat food, toys, and even clothes.

Kiki – big, white, and fluffy – sat demurely at Mother's feet. Mother could hear Father on the phone and called out to him now while he spoke to Wendy.

"Send her my love!" she called, and then blew her nose loudly like a little trumpet. Father turned from the kitchen to wave at Mother. He smiled at her and blew her a kiss with his hand and she pretended to catch it, her handkerchief still waving in her hand.

She held the imaginary kiss against her chest in a clenched fist, the handkerchief now sticking out from between her fingers. They really were a soppy pair.

"Mother sends her love, dear!" said Father, turning back to the kitchen.

"Thanks," Wendy said flatly. She looked down at the cat basket by her side.

The cat's green eyes peered out at her. Wendy wasn't happy. She really didn't want to take Grandma's cat home with her.

"Maybe you should just take the cat to a shelter, Wendy. Honestly, that's what they're there for," Dad repeated, now whisking some eggs as he spoke.

"But Dad . . ."

"Listen, Wendy," Dad said, interrupting Wendy. "I have to go. The regional judge – Mrs Fowler – is coming over in twenty minutes for breakfast with us, so we need to get ready." He continued whisking the eggs in a glass bowl whilst looking on the kitchen shelf for some herbs, the phone tucked against his shoulder.

"Dad, I . . ." Wendy tried to interrupt her father, but it was no good. She felt her heart begin to race as she stared at the cat basket. Dad seemed not to hear her as he continued talking over her.

"Mrs Fowler thinks Martha and Kiki have what it takes to go all the way to the top – *the very top!* I don't want to speak too soon, but there's been talk of a show on TV where the cats meet celebrities!" He was now really excited about Martha and Kiki and had forgotten what they were actually talking about. Wendy wanted to bring him back onto the topic of Grandma's cat – and fast.

"That's great, Dad, and with this . . . nice cat . . . can't you take it permanently? I mean, you did have her for a couple of weeks, didn't you?"

14

Wendy didn't think the cat was nice at all, but wanted to encourage her father to take it.

Her father frowned, thinking about the cat. "I'm sorry, Wendy, that one's a *mongrel* – we really cannot take the risk with *our* cats." He looked over his shoulder to Mother, who was now sitting completely upright as though she had a wooden plank stuck to her back. She shook her head vigorously "no" and the living room armchair seemed to shake with her.

He continued, trying to be a little more gentle. "Wendy, when we took Grandma's cat in, it was an emergency – she was in hospital. It was the right thing to do. But now: no. You know, the whole time we had that cat at our house, we actually had to keep our cats separate from it, just in case. We really can't live like that. Listen, we left her there for you today – because that's what Grandma *really* would have wanted. A little friend for you."

Wendy's mother interrupted again. "Tell her . . ."

Dad turned around, a little bit startled by her voice, and the egg he was whisking almost slopped out of the bowl.

"Sorry, dear, what was that?" he replied with a smile.

Wendy thought her father was talking to her. "I don't need a little friend, Dad, what I need is . . ."

Mum called over to Dad, "What she needs is a man!"

Wendy couldn't make out what her mother was saying, but she could hear her father loudly clearing his throat. It was obvious that her mother had said something inflammatory, as she often tended to do. Wendy went silent. She felt like yelling down the phone at her parents, but instead, she just about managed to keep her cool.

"Did you hear your mother, dear?" Dad asked Wendy earnestly.

Wendy closed her eyes and breathed in deeply, trying not to get angry. "No, Dad, but I was thinking – as I don't have a boyfriend, maybe I can just bring the cat to lunch with me next

Sunday – seeing how she's my *new friend*," Wendy said sarcastically. She was sure that her mother's comment had been something about a boyfriend – it always was. Her mum was like a broken record.

"Well, let's just stick to people, shall we?" Dad replied jovially. Wendy narrowed her eyes angrily as her father continued speaking without taking a breath. "Oh! Speaking of people, Grandma's gnome is yours," he laughed, talking to himself, "with that funny red hat – what a character!"

"Dad!" Wendy tried to interrupt.

"Anyway, right, we need to get going. As I said, the judge will be here any minute now. OK dear, well, bye-bye, see you for lunch next Sunday!"

"But Dad!" Wendy exclaimed as the phone line went dead.

She looked at her phone in disbelief for a second and then shoved it into her pocket, frowning in annoyance at the situation.

Feeling utterly deflated, she looked down at the cat basket next to her. A pair of green eyes had been watching her while she had been speaking on the phone, and now they looked up at her, timidly, as if enquiring what she was going to do next. Wendy sighed heavily, looking at the cat.

"I can't stand cats," she said, stooping to pick up the basket. As she did, a loud crash resounded through the house and she jumped backwards in shock, grasping at thin air as she moved, and completely missing the cat basket's handle.

"Sorry!" called the muffled voice of one of the removal men upstairs.

Wendy took a breath in, recovering from the shock. "Great, it's like Humpty Dumpty in here," she muttered, shaking her head. It felt like everything was going wrong today.

This reminded her that she had agreed to meet her oddball of a boss at the office today to pick up an important package. Hastily, she checked the time on her watch; she needed to get a move on. She picked up the cat basket and began to walk slightly lopsidedly - the basket was so heavy! She looked a little bit like the *Leaning Tower of Pisa* as she walked, tilted to one side, trying to carry the weighty cat basket, the time now against her.

She moved quickly down the hallway towards the front door, trying not to tip the basket too much. It wasn't easy with the heavy box of keepsakes under one arm and the heavy wicker cat basket in the other hand. As she walked she noticed that her shoelace was dragging. She rolled her eyes – yet another annoyance. She blew her auburn hair from her eyes.

She gently set down the cat basket and the keepsake box with the vase, tucked her hair behind her ear, and began to tie her shoelace. Behind her in the hallway, a removal man appeared, clasping a large painting in a heavy golden frame.

"Excuse me!" he said, puffing. His cheeks were red and he strained with the bulky weight of the painting.

Wendy calmly continued to tie her shoelace, completely unaware that the man was waiting for her to move. Sweat trickled down his face as he glared at the back of her head.

"I said, excuse me!" he repeated, urgently.

Wendy finished tying her shoelace and only then did she notice the man standing there. His face was as red as a beet at this point. She was surprised to see him there! She stood and turned to look at him, smiling awkwardly, not sure what was happening. Perhaps he needed her help, she thought. He glared back at her.

"Are you deaf or something?" he said, annoyed, as he struggled past with the painting.

Wendy felt very hurt; her face went red and her stomach churned. She picked up the cat basket and her box and rushed out of the house as fast as possible.

As she made her way to her car, the man's rude comment and angry red face played out in her mind on repeat. She was due to receive important test results the next day regarding her hearing and, in her mind, everything hinged on them.

As she left Grandma's house for the last time, her heart felt heavy and the man's comment really hurt her. She just wanted to feel "normal," whatever that was.

Once Wendy was inside her small car and she had secured the cat basket in the back seat with a seat belt, she began to drive. The privacy and quiet of her car felt good and the road seemed to clear her thinking a little as she drove. She straightened up in her seat and breathed out. She needed to focus on getting to work now. She was already late – she had so much to do!

As she drove, she looked back at the cat in the car mirror. The basket bounced on the back seat and the cat sat hunched, like a little brown ball.

That cat didn't want *her* to keep it – that seemed clear. *What interest does it have in me?* she thought to herself as she drove. It clearly didn't like her, she could tell already. It would much rather be with someone else – a cat person – someone who actually likes cats and has time for one.

Wendy brought her eyes back to the road. One thing was for sure: whatever happened, she would *not* be keeping the cat.

CHAPTER 3

A Plan

Wendy drove fast along the country roads as rain splashed heavily against her windscreen. The countryside seemed to disappear in a blur. She wanted to get everything done at the office so that she could then focus her attention on finding a new home for the cat.

Suddenly, a bird swooped low in front of the car and Wendy jumped on the brakes, narrowly avoiding the bird. In the back of the car the little cat went flying into the side of her wicker basket with a thud. The cat looked out at Wendy with a glare. Her furry face was crumpled against the wicker – she was not a happy cat.

"Sorry!" Wendy called back to the cat, regaining her composure. The little cat shook her head and fluffed up her fur, settling herself back in the middle of the basket.

Wendy continued to drive at a slightly slower speed and called to the "hands free" system in her car. She needed to call her boss, Bryan, and let him know that she was going to be late.

"Call Bryan!" Wendy shouted at the car and it connected to her phone.

A ring tone started to buzz from the car's speakers and Wendy turned up the volume.

"Wendaline!" Bryan answered enthusiastically, yelling into his phone. He was so loud that Wendy and the cat both jumped and Wendy quickly turned down the volume. Bryan always over-compensated for the fact that Wendy was losing her hearing. He would shout at Wendy as though he were speaking above loud music.

"Good to hear you!" his voice boomed from the car speakers. "Is everything OK?"

Wendy shook her head, trying not to laugh at how silly Bryan sounded yelling at his phone.

"Yes, thank you, Bryan, I just wanted to let you know that I'm going to be twenty minutes late. Something has come up."

"OK, no problem, I understand – with your grandma and your family. See you when you get here!"

"See you then."

Wendy hung up and continued driving. She narrowed her eyes with resolve. She was determined to get rid of the cat and would have to come up with a plan very soon.

On the back seat, the little cat bumped around in her basket, watching Wendy as she drove. The cat wrapped her tail around her body like a little scarf and fluffed up her fur with resolve: she knew that Wendy wanted to get rid of her but she had other ideas.

In fact, the cat knew Wendy well. She had watched her grow into an adult. Wendy had never really petted her or spoken to her, but she had watched Wendy with Grandma baking and making crafts, and she liked her. She let out a small inaudible sigh and Wendy's eyes flicked into her car mirror, looking at the cat as if sensing her thoughts.

"We'll find you a home, don't you worry," Wendy said to the cat, her eyes flicking back to the road.

The cat moved her eyes from Wendy to the inside of her wicker basket as she keenly studied the latch which secured the basket door. There was a gap between the basket's door and the latch which fastened it. She studied this with a look of great curiosity in her green eyes; little did Wendy know that the cat was formulating a plan all of her own.

The cat seemed to think for a moment, and then snuggled down deeper into the purple blanket inside the basket. She had decided to make the most of this very difficult situation. What else could a small cat do? She was at the mercy of those around her.

Despite all of this uncertainty and Wendy's, frankly, hectic driving, there was a deep sense of calm about this cat, as though she was staring fate in the eye.

Her green eyes glittered, shining like beautiful emeralds, and anyone watching this nondescript, small, quiet cat would have to admit that, in that moment, there was something magical about her.

Soon, after yet more bumping and Wendy playing around with the radio until she grew bored of it, the car came to a stop in a small carpark in front of a newly-built, red brick building. It was surrounded by fields, just outside of town. Wendy quickly got out of the car, locking the doors.

The cat watched Wendy as her auburn hair blew in the wind and she marched across the tarmacked carpark, disappearing into the building.

Inside the building, Wendy climbed a short staircase up to Bryan's office and stopped at a pine door facing the top of the stairs. On the door a shiny silver plaque shone, engraved with the words:

BRYAN BROGAN WEB DESIGN

Wendy politely knocked twice on the door and then opened it.

"Hi Bryan!" she said breezily, putting on her best smile. She didn't want to talk to him about her morning and thought that playing happy was the best way to avoid any awkward questions; he could be annoyingly intrusive at times.

Inside, the office was small and bright, with enough room for two people, and Bryan sat at his desk behind two side-by-side computer screens, his face illuminated by their light. His black-rimmed glasses shone like mirrors, obscuring his eyes behind them as he clicked impatiently on the computer's mouse.

He was so engrossed in what he was doing that he didn't immediately react to Wendy's entrance. He was staring at something on the screen and, all the while, his pink tongue meandered slightly from the corner of his mouth. Finally, he became aware that there was someone there and, even though he was slightly startled, he made it a point to look up at Wendy slowly and nonchalantly, attempting to mask his surprise.

"This mouse is jumping around like a wet kipper! I think I need to update the software. I can't seem to place anything on the screen where I want it!" he exclaimed to Wendy, bypassing any pleasantries and frowning. He raised a mug with a picture of a spaceship to his mouth, took a big slurp, and sighed loudly.

As he put the mug down, some cocoa was left on his top lip. It looked like a big moustache. Bryan was nearly old enough to retire, but it didn't stop him from acting as though he were a toddler.

"Oh, really? Well, the sensor may just need a clean," Wendy replied politely in response to Bryan's comment about the mouse. She looked at the chocolate around Bryan's mouth and stopped herself from laughing. "You, um. . ." She gestured to her mouth, indicating to Bryan that he had something there, and he swiped away the chocolate with the back of his hand.

"Thanks!" Bryan said, looking at the chocolate on the back of his hand. "Where would I be without my Wendaline!"

Wendy shrugged, frowning as she watched him wipe his hand inside his jacket.

"You know," he continued in an animated fashion, "they say that true friends tell their friends when they have food on their face. I guess that makes you a real star, Wendy!"

"Thanks Bryan. It's really noth –"

"Anyway," he interrupted, cracking his fingers in front of him like they were made from little twigs.

"Your NEW PHONE HAS COME!" he suddenly shouted, over-accentuating his mouth so that each word was so clear you could tell what he was saying across a football stadium.

"Uh, I really need to learn to speak up around you, sorry. I wasn't speaking very CLEARLY BEFORE!" He continued shouting. "I JUST KEEP FORGETTING! IT'S NOT LIKE YOU CAN SEE THAT THERE'S ANYTHING WRONG, SORRY!"

"Right," Wendy said, crossing her arms – she felt angry and awkward. "Bryan, there isn't anything 'wrong' with me as you put it, there isn't anything 'wrong' at all! And I can understand you perfectly well without the insane shouting, thank you."

"Oh, OK, sorry." Bryan made the action of a zip with his fingers across his mouth as though silencing himself. "Didn't mean to offend you, old girl. You know what I'm like – foot in mouth syndrome. Just ignore it." He patted the desk, smiling weakly at Wendy and laughing awkwardly.

"So," Wendy continued, choosing to ignore the spectacle that Bryan had just made of himself – as usual. "My new phone has arrived today!" She tried to sound cheery.

"Yes, yes!" Bryan said, smiling. He made a drum roll on his desk with his fingers and then reached dramatically underneath the desk, pulling up a large box which he rotated in the air with his hands while making spaceship noises.

"It's here!" he exclaimed.

On the side of the box was a brightly coloured photograph of an elderly man smiling out at her as he used a phone connected to a small computer-like screen. Bryan thrust the box forward at Wendy, and the old man's face loomed closer. The whole intolerably embarrassing scene made Wendy want to disappear from the room.

"Ta-daah! This is great! I practically had to tear it away from my kids." Bryan grinned broadly, pleased with himself.

Wendy looked at Bryan with a hurt look on her face. He mistook her look as concern for his disappointed children.

"Oh, don't worry, they'll get over it!" he said, grinning.

"Great" Wendy said, downcast.

"Sorry, did I get the wrong colour?" He turned the box in his hands awkwardly, squinting at the writing on the box, examining each side to see where it indicated the colour of the phone.

"It says silver here," he said finally, prodding the box with a stubby finger.

"No, it's not that . . . it's – it's great, thank you. Really." Wendy breathed out through her nose, letting out a sigh. There was no point in telling him that he had offended her – and she didn't want the confrontation. It was just embarrassing.

"That's my Wendaline!" he said, smiling, and leant across his desk, handing the phone to her.

As he reached across the desk, a leaflet, which had been perched on top of the desk, caught his jacket cuff and fluttered to the floor. Wendy bent and picked it up.

On the front of the leaflet, a smiling lady wearing a blue uniform was sitting in a wide green field with a dog, a cat, a rabbit, and a rooster. At the top of the leaflet were the words:

Loving Hearts Animal Sanctuary

Wendy placed the leaflet back on Bryan's desk.

"Have you been here before?" she enquired, taking the phone from Bryan.

"Not yet – it's the local one, you know –"

"Yes, near town," Wendy replied eagerly. "Would you mind if I take this?" She looked at the front of the leaflet and the happy scene it depicted.

Bryan nodded with a grin. "No, go ahead! I've got another one at home. Thinking of adopting, are we?" Bryan said, grinning broadly again, his teeth like neat white rectangles of marble.

"Well . . ." Wendy smiled, moving her head from side to side as if it was something she was weighing up.

"Best way, really," Bryan said, leaning back in his chair with an air of knowing. "Let me tell you, my kids are obsessed with getting a Corgi – like the Queen has. I figured this was a good way to get one on discount – if you know what I mean."

Bryan laughed loudly at his own joke, his glasses reflecting the bright office lights above like mirrors as he tilted his head back, giggling.

Wendy raised an eyebrow at him, then looked down at the phone in her hands and thought about the cat sitting in her car. Suddenly she felt like she couldn't cope with everything all at once.

The sanctuary on the leaflet would be her best bet, she thought. They could take the cat and she could get on with her life.

"Anyway," Bryan said, clapping his hands together, "it's always good to talk, but we'd better get moving." He looked at his computer screen and whistled to himself. "Well, well, we've just received confirmation for an order that's come in from a band. I figured you'd be into that, music buff that you are." He smiled, slurping at his cocoa again, coming away with a giant moustache above his lip.

Wendy looked up at a poster on the wall behind Bryan. She had looked at it many times in the past, yet today it perfectly summed up how she was feeling. Garfield the cat held a chainsaw, aiming it at a computer whilst yelling, "*COMPUTE THIS!*"

She looked at Bryan and pursed her lips. "That's good about the website." She attempted a smile, but it came out as a kind of half smile, with just one corner of her mouth rising slightly. Bryan patted his desk with a large hand and then gestured to the door with a stubby finger.

"Well, what's stopping you?" He exclaimed with a grin.

"Yes, right, well I'd better get this thing set up then," Wendy replied, holding up the phone. She turned to leave, happy to be getting away from Bryan. As she reached the office door, Bryan quickly pulled a whistle from his desk drawer. Before Wendy had time to get through the door, he was blowing into the whistle with all his might, his cheeks puffing out like a red balloon.

"Wheeeee!" it rang out, its tinny sound piercing the quiet air.

Wendy jolted on the spot and she turned to glare at Bryan, unable to comprehend what on Earth he was doing.

"Go for gold!" he yelled. "The whistle is for encouragement, you know, to put a little spring in your step! I use it on my kids when it's time for bed – works on everyone!"

Wendy took a deep breath and then regained her composure. "I see. I think my heart just stopped, actually," she said, turning back to the door and shaking her head in bewilderment.

Bryan really was one of the strangest people she had ever met. He meant well, but when it came to people skills, he really had a long way to go. Still, she liked him – most of the time.

CHAPTER 4

The Shelter

As Wendy made her way to the animal shelter, lightning forked
down into a field in the distance with a crash and the cat hun-
kered down in her basket.

The car was crammed with papers from Wendy's work, the box
of keepsakes, the phone, and on the back seat, the cat in her basket
– there was barely room to breathe. The car's little wipers worked
frantically, beating left then right, wiping the water from the wind-
shield in what sounded like a squeaking fury.

Wendy couldn't wait to get to the animal sanctuary, give them the
cat, and forget that this morning had ever happened.

She was so busy happily anticipating unloading the cat at the
shelter that she almost missed the turn for the actual animal shelter!
She pulled the car's wheel sharply to the left, narrowly avoiding a
very wet and bedraggled cyclist, who angrily waved a fluorescent-
gloved fist at her.

As a result, once again, the poor cat went sliding to the other
side of the car as though she were on ice, and her basket bumped

up against the car's plastic interior. The cat looked sharply out of the basket at Wendy. Her whiskers seemed to twitch this time.

"Sorry!" Wendy called out to the cat again. Even though she didn't like cats, she wasn't mean. She was just in a hurry to get on with her life.

Slowly now, she drove the small blue car along a rough gravel road that led to the animal shelter. The road was very uneven and the small car bumped along over large stones and into deep pot holes, rattling up and down. It was a real boneshaker.

In the basket on the back seat, the cat bounced up and down like a fluffy tennis ball. Water splashed from the potholes in the road and sprayed up against the sides of the car, coating it in a fine layer of sticky mud. The little cat continued to bounce and rattle along with the car; she felt like a pair of shaking maracas. She was not a happy cat.

Finally, Wendy brought the car to a halt near a small strip of grass and breathed a sigh of relief as she switched off the engine. She could see that, nearby, round stone slabs led across the grass to a white rectangular office building. Attached to the slate roof of the building, there was a large, eggshell-blue sign. Bright white lettering seemed to shine out in the grey sky:

Loving Hearts Animal Sanctuary
Reception

Wendy pulled the wicker cat basket from the car and walked towards the reception building, awkwardly carrying the heavy basket at her side. She struggled to get through the heavy glass reception door. In the end she was forced to put the cat basket down, open the door, and keep it held open with her foot. She grabbed the basket with both hands and staggered through the door.

Finally, she was inside the sanctuary reception building; it wouldn't be long before she would be able to say goodbye to the cat – and then get on with her life.

It was warm inside the building, and it smelled of straw and dogs. There were coloured pencils and stationery for sale on the wooden counter and, at one side in the corner of the room, there was an area with animal baskets, treats, leashes, and collars and all kinds of pet care equipment for new pet owners to purchase.

I won't be needing any of that, Wendy thought. She reached the empty reception desk and peered over, and the cat shuffled nervously in her basket.

Wendy rang a large brass bell on the counter, hitting it urgently twice… and then a third time for good measure. She was in no mood for this. She had imagined happy volunteers with big smiles, rushing to take the cat basket away from her.

She grew even more impatient as the seconds ticked by.

"Hello! Is anyone there?" she called loudly, ringing the desk bell again and leaning over further to look.

A young man stepped out from a door next to the reception. He was wearing a blue polo shirt with a badge pinned to it that was shaped like a cat's head. The badge said VOLUNTEER.

"Hello! Sorry, we're really busy!" he said, smiling as he rushed to the reception desk.

Wendy hoisted the large wicker cat basket onto the reception desk with the cat peering out from inside. Wendy breathed a sigh of relief as she put the basket in place. She barely looked at the man as she began to speak quickly.

"I just really need your help," she said shaking her head at her feet, thinking of her morning. "This morning, rather surprisingly, things took a turn for the unexpected, you see . . ." She paused for a moment now. She hadn't thought about how she was going to explain why she couldn't take the cat herself. "I, um . . . happened upon this cat." She gestured to the cat basket with an open palm, making her most honest face as she did.

Simon opened the cat basket and the cat stepped forward timidly. Her paws left sweaty prints on the reception desk because she was really nervous now.

"OK, let's have a look," Simon said, taking a pair of glasses from his pocket and placing them upon his nose. He looked at Wendy properly this time.

Wow, she's beautiful! he thought.

"I'm Simon, by the way." He held out his hand.

Wendy shook his hand and looked into his green eyes. She thought that he was very handsome and this made her feel shy. She focused on the cat standing on the table, not wanting Simon to notice her shyness.

"I'm Wendy," she said, trying to be cool.

"Where did you find . . ." Simon took the cat and revolved it on the table, lifting its tail to see if it was a boy or a girl. Wendy wasn't sure what he was doing at first. "*Her*," Simon concluded. "*She* . . . is a girl."

Wendy already knew this and – feeling awkward – politely pretended to be surprised by this revelation. "Oh, she was – well, she belonged to my grandmother."

"I see," Simon murmured in a slightly judgmental way.

"I really can't keep her and I was hoping that you could help me here," Wendy said looking at the ground once she had finished speaking. She felt very uncomfortable. She had been straining sometimes to hear what he had been saying and now she was forced to tell him the truth about where the cat had come from.

"We're full, I'm afraid. There are just too many stray animals and not enough homes for them," Simon said, sighing. "We're only a small shelter and we rely entirely on donations – which means we only have the ability to take emergency cases right now."

Wendy nodded. She understood the point about their priorities: there may be other animals needing help – the ones with no hope. But, to her, *this was an emergency.*

Simon took off his glasses and cleared his throat.

"But," he continued, "you should keep calling us here at the shelter and, if anything changes, I will definitely let you know. We may have a space opening up in the next day – one of our longest residents, Mr. Bojangles."

Wendy raised an eyebrow quizzically.

"He's a Siamese cat," Simon quickly clarified. "He might have found a home – at last. In any event, I might be able to help you –"

Just then, a teenage colleague of Simon's – her name was Sally and everyone knew her around the shelter as she was quite nosey – came bursting into the reception area through a side door.

"It's time for your break, Simon! That disgusting egg sandwich of yours is ready from the microwave. All of the dogs know it already!" Sally yelled, laughing.

Simon looked embarrassed.

"Sorry about that," he said to Wendy, his cheeks flushing. "Like I said, we may get a space very soon, and then I could help you with the cat."

Sally noticed Simon and Wendy smiling at each other and she could tell that he liked Wendy.

"Listen," Sally said, barging in. "If you need some help finding someone for the cat," Sally flicked her hair back dramatically, then turned and tore a piece of paper from a pad and quickly scrawled a number on it, "give us a call here, OK?"

Wendy took the piece of paper from Sally without looking at it.

"OK, thank you," she said, stepping towards the door. She needed to get going. She had so much work to do with the web design orders that Bryan had sent her, and the shelter had been no good – she still had the cat.

With one hand holding the cat basket and her elbow pressing against the reception door, Wendy took the piece of paper from Sally and placed it between her lips.

"Bye!" Wendy said in a muffled call, the paper moving in her mouth as she spoke. She headed back out towards her car, carrying the cat basket in both hands. As she walked away, Simon watched her and sighed.

What Wendy and Simon *hadn't* realised was that Sally had been sneaky. Back inside the shelter reception, Simon seemed confused now.

"Why didn't you give her our business card? Why did you write the number on that slip of paper – was it the right one?" He looked concerned.

Sally rolled her eyes and smiled mischievously.

"Calm down and think about it, Sherlock. The shelter business card doesn't have your personal number on it, does it? I know it off by heart, from all the times I've had to call you from the office phone about pet care stuff."

Sally was clearly pleased with herself. She laughed and skipped back through the side door, leaving Simon alone in the reception.

Simon felt disappointed and a bit confused. He wondered whether he would ever see Wendy and the cat again. He wished he had been bolder – maybe he could have found a way to talk to Wendy some more. He really hoped he would see her again, but Wendy was in such a hurry to leave at the end, he wasn't sure. He was worried about the cat too – where would *she* go next? A lot of the animal shelters around were "kill shelters" – sometimes they only gave cats a few days to find a home, and he hadn't had the time to tell Wendy about this before she had rushed out the door.

CHAPTER 5

A New Friend

Finally, Wendy arrived home. It had been a long and busy morning and, now that she had collected the text phone from Bryan, she had to set it up. She walked into her living room and, with a sigh of relief, set down the box of items from Grandma's house – which now included the text phone – and placed the cat basket next to it. It was good to put everything down for a moment and she gave her body a shake to let out some of the tension. She picked up the text phone from the box.

Wendy looked at the cat in her basket.

"Right, don't go anywhere, I'll just be a moment," she said sarcastically. *As if a cat can understand me*, Wendy thought as she climbed the stairs to her office. Once inside her small office with its blue polka dot curtains and antique writing desk, Wendy looked again at the phone's box and shook her head. An elderly man on the box grinned ecstatically while using the text phone. "I'm not geriatric," Wendy said out loud, deflated.

In the photo, there was text displayed on the phone's large screen, and the old man was reading what it said. The phone's screen read: *Hello Dave.*

Wendy wasn't sure she would be as happy as the old man to use the phone – his smile went practically from ear to ear. She shook her head again, as this time she thought of Bryan. He always shouted when speaking to her; she didn't think she would need to read what he was saying from the phone's screen just yet. He could probably be heard by his entire neighbourhood!

The thing was, even with the text phone, Wendy wasn't sure when Bryan would finally "get the message" that he didn't need to shout at her to be understood.

Wendy sighed, looking at her desk and the new phone now upon it. It was a clear sign that things were changing. She decided not to set up the phone just then, as she felt depressed by it. She didn't want to think about the ways in which her life was changing – and it just served to bring her confidence down.

She didn't want to be judged, to suddenly be deemed somehow "less able" than she was before. She hated this kind of judgment. But what she couldn't see was that *she* was becoming the harshest judge of them all – her own worst critic.

She walked back down the small cream-carpeted stairs from her office and into the living room to check on the cat. Before she even reached the cat basket, she could see that its door was wide open. The basket sat facing her; it was completely empty. The cat was an escape artist! A feline Houdini!

"Oh, come on!" Wendy said to herself, exasperated in disbelief.

Her eyes travelled to the open window in her living room – that was where the cat must have gone! She opened the small door that connected her living room to the back garden and stepped out onto her patio. It felt cold underfoot in just her socks.

She could see the cat ahead of her, its tail swaying behind it like a feather duster as it moved quickly towards the small black gate at the side of the house. It slipped under the gate with ease and continued down the side of the house on her way to the street.

As the cat heard Wendy approaching her, she began to scamper. Wendy jogged after the cat. As Wendy reached the side gate, she opened it quickly and stepped through. Her socked feet met crunchy gravel, making her walk and hop awkwardly as though hot coals lined her path. The cat swiftly reached the street ahead of her and disappeared around the corner and out of Wendy's sight.

"Oh, no!" Wendy said with dismay, chasing around the corner in hot pursuit of the cat. As she rounded the corner, the cat came into view – she looked back at Wendy, blinking nonchalantly. The cat had been walking slowly, stalling for time, and was now standing just a few feet from her. Wendy wondered what the cat's game was. It was acting all innocent – it just stood there, looking up at her, blinking.

"Here Kitty-Cat! Here Kitty!" Wendy tried to use her best "nice person" voice so that the cat would stop running from her. She also reached her hand out to touch the cat, edging closer to it.

"Oh, come on – please!" Wendy called, as the cat zoomed away just as she almost touched it. The cat would allow her to get close to it and then suddenly speed up, its paws moving fast so that she had no chance to catch it. It was clear to Wendy that the cat wanted her to follow it. *But why?* Its fluffy tail bounced along in front of her, luring her further.

Wendy followed the cat as she continued up the street to a small white bungalow which was two houses up the street from Wendy's small house. The bungalow had a neat front garden and a small concrete birdbath. There was a large FOR SALE sign hammered into the lawn. Across the sign, a red banner declared the property SOLD in large white letters.

"You can't go there – this isn't your house!" Wendy whispered loudly to the cat, who now ran to the front door of the house.

This house belonged to Mrs Budnick, a new neighbour of Wendy's. She was a kindly older lady who had just returned to Sunnymede after spending a number of years back in her home country of Ukraine.

Wendy had only spoken to Mrs Budnick a few times, and now here she was, standing beside the cat who sat in a determined stance on Mrs Budnick's doormat! Wendy sighed and, exasperated, she went over to where the cat was sitting at the front door.

"Are you happy now? Let's go," Wendy said, bending down to pick up the cat.

Suddenly the door swung open and Wendy jumped, startled, as Mrs Budnick took a step forward from her doorway. Mrs Budnick gasped as the cat bolted through her stockinged legs and straight into her house! Wendy's face went bright red as she met Mrs Budnick's bespectacled wide eyes.

"Oh my goodness!" Mrs Budnick cried, almost falling backwards.

CHAPTER 6

Matinka Budnick

Mrs Budnick stood with her hands on her hips as Wendy apologised to her profusely. They stood in Mrs Budnick's living room where the cat had made herself comfortable in an armchair and now slept soundly.

"Wendy, please stop apologising," Mrs Budnick said, smiling now. "It is no problem; I open the door to get paper – I get cat – two for one!"

Mrs Budnick laughed at her own joke. She had a strong accent and Wendy had to concentrate hard to hear her and understand her.

Wendy looked around Mrs Budnick's living room: the walls had been newly papered with light floral wallpaper. On the oval dining table, a vase of flowers was positioned over a large white embroidered tablecloth to cover the varnished wood. There was a basket with painted eggs inside it on a small side dresser, and a miniature blue-and-gold flag of Ukraine poked out from the basket. The painted eggs looked beautiful and intricate, Wendy thought, as she glanced over at them.

"Sorry! I am so sorry about this!" Wendy said again, shuffling her feet with embarrassment.

Mrs Budnick patted Wendy on the shoulder gently and raised her eyebrow, noticing the fact that Wendy had no shoes on, but was too polite to comment. At least Wendy was wearing socks – nice ones, rainbow-coloured.

"Ah, she make decision, it is fine. It has been many years since I had kittsya – I mean, cat."

Wendy had been learning to read lips to help with her hearing loss and Mrs Budnick was a good candidate for her to practice her new skill on.

Wendy concentrated very hard on Mrs Budnick's mouth as she spoke, as she didn't have much experience yet. She watched the shapes Mrs Budnick's full, neat mouth made as words tumbled from her lipstick-pink lips. It was a great skill for Wendy to acquire and she had learned that a person who can read lips can tell what anyone is saying from a distance or up close, even if they cannot hear them.

"Are you sure it's OK?" Wendy said, trying to hide her relief.

"Yes, dear. I did not have cat in Ukraine. My grandchildren are my pets. I miss cats. This will be good, I love cat! My nephew will love her. He loves all animals! But my son, Olek, he is different story. He has many allergies – but he leave earlier, so is good now."

Wendy couldn't believe her luck. It was like everything had just fallen into place.

"Thank you so much, Mrs Budnick!" She felt like hugging her but held back and just smiled instead.

Mrs Budnick patted her shoulder again. "Well, it is not a problem. But Olek is back on Friday. So then, I have to say goodbye to cat."

"OK, that isn't a problem!" Wendy said enthusiastically. This would give her a little bit of time to find the cat a place to live and then she wouldn't have to see it again. "Friday," she repeated, and Mrs Budnick nodded an emphatic "yes."

Mrs Budnick paused and looked at Wendy closely.

"How is your hearing?"

Wendy was a little taken aback at this question and felt embarrassed. But she quickly decided not to avoid the question, as Mrs

Budnick didn't mean anything bad by it; she was just a very straightforward kind of woman.

"Oh, I'm fine. How do you know I can't hear very well?" Wendy said, raising an eyebrow.

"Ah, it takes one to know one." Mrs Budnick gestured to her own hearing aid behind her ear. "I watch people's lips too; it is how we listen."

Wendy forced a small smile onto her face. She felt awkward, and Mrs Budnick could tell.

"Well, I'm fine. It's all OK," Wendy said, trying to sound bright and breezy. "Anyway, thank you so much for saying that you will take the cat for now. I know you haven't lived here long and you're still settling in. I really appreciate it and I'm sorry she just ran in like that."

"Ah, that is no problem at all, I have room." Mrs Budnick leant forward and gave Wendy a hug now, squeezing her a little. Wendy could smell Mrs Budnick's perfume and the smell of clean fresh soapsuds. It reminded her of her grandma and she felt sad.

Mrs Budnick stepped back and looked at Wendy, remembering something.

"Since you are here, I want to tell you. I was going to post you a note – to ask will you come to my birthday – on Saturday?"

Wendy smiled. She liked Mrs Budnick; she was happy to be invited to her birthday party.

"It is just a small party, some food, a few guests, nothing big." Mrs Budnick looked to Wendy expectantly.

"Oh, I would love to," Wendy said smiling. "That sounds great, thank you. And thank you for looking after the cat. I promise I'll find her a home. I just have to get back to work for now. But I will definitely find her a home."

"Of course and, for now, I will be Kitty's foster matinka – that's mother, dear. She has what name?"

Wendy looked down at the floor. She didn't want to say.

"It's Wendy."

"No, the cat, dear." Mrs Budnick looked confused.

"That *is* her name – my grandmother named her after me."

Mrs Budnick looked thoughtful.

"OK, you go work now." Mrs Budnick touched Wendy's cheek kindly. "You are good girl, you know. Be happy."

Wendy smiled a little sadly, followed Mrs Budnick to the front door, and said goodbye. As she walked back to her house, Wendy still didn't know how she was going to find the cat a home. Losing her hearing was life-changing.

Everything was shifting around her and sometimes she felt overwhelmed thinking about the future. Her footsteps somehow felt heavy as she returned to her front door.

As a way of coping, Wendy had taken on more and more work to try to bury her emotions. It was her way of distracting herself from her feelings; she didn't have time to think about them. With such a full work schedule, she didn't have a lot of time to find a home for the cat either.

She had recently taken on several new web design projects. She was working on more things at once than she had ever done before and, outside of work, she was taking intensive classes for sign language and lip reading. Wendy put a lot of pressure on herself because it bothered her when she didn't know the right sign or gesture. She wanted to be able to be fluent in sign language. She already knew a little bit from spending time with her grandmother, but her grandmother's situation was different in that she had lost her hearing later in life and preferred to read people's lips.

In the meantime, she had to get her new phone up and running and figure out how it worked.

Some days she felt like she was climbing a giant mountain, as she prepared herself for a future without hearing.

Inside her house, Wendy sat at her office desk. She looked at the phone's large box and a pang of anxiety ran through her. It was a fact that, even as time passed, Wendy still held a hope in her heart that she might be able to halt her hearing loss. Recently, she had visited a specialist ear doctor who had told her some very promising information. He had said that it might be possible to stop her condition from taking her hearing completely. This possibility had excited her.

She was finally due to receive the doctor's test results the next day. This gave her some hope. Wendy mulled things over in her mind. The only problem was – what if there wasn't anything that the doctor could do?

CHAPTER 7

The Doctor's Office

Wendy sat waiting inside the doctor's office. A receptionist with a shiny black bob hairstyle and deep red lipstick had led her to the office. Her black patent leather shoes clip-clopped down the marble-floored hallway before she stopped at a white door. She had opened it and told Wendy to take a seat; the doctor would be with her shortly.

Now Wendy sat alone in a plastic, red, faux leather chair that squeaked every time she moved. The room smelled of disinfectant and a clock tapped on the wall.

She looked curiously at a giant model of the human ear, which sat on the doctor's desk in front of her. The office walls were covered with posters showing smiling people wearing hearing aids. Most of the people in the photos were much older than Wendy – which added to her growing feelings of discomfort.

The door behind Wendy opened and Dr. Burton – a stern looking man in his late fifties who had a large black moustache and, other than that, only about three hairs remaining on his head – strode into the room. Wendy had wondered to herself if the large moustache was to compensate for the lack of hair on his head.

Wendy turned awkwardly in the squeaky chair as he walked in behind her. He dried his hands on a piece of blue towel paper and opened the garbage can next to his desk with a clang, throwing it inside.

He sat down, still looking stern and, without introduction, he began:

"Wendy, I have some news for you and it may not be what you were hoping to . . . er . . ."

Wendy realised the error that Dr. Burton had made in the way he phrased his sentence.

". . . hear?" Wendy finished the sentence for him in a matter-of-fact way.

Dr. Burton didn't smile. He tapped his fingers on the desk for a second, thinking before continuing.

"The molecular genetic testing we conducted, coupled with our knowledge of your grandmother's loss of hearing indicates that . . ."

Wendy cut into what Dr. Burton was saying. She didn't like what he had to say so far. It didn't make much sense – the "molecular" whatever it was – and his depressing tone. She was here to be positive. To find a solution.

"Well, yes, the tests," Wendy said, trying to redirect the conversation. "So there IS something you can do – a new trial, or a medication or something right?"

Dr. Burton tilted his head down, looking at Wendy as though down the length of his nose, as though it were a telescope that would help him to see better.

"I'm sorry, Wendy. It's just a matter of time now until you lose your hearing completely. It's irreversible, a one-way street, I'm afraid."

Wendy felt her stomach sink. It felt as though all of her energy drained out of her and into a black pool beneath her somewhere. She breathed in and then let the air out slowly, gathering her thoughts.

"Right," she said, trying not to cry. She managed to keep a calm face, but inside she just wanted to find somewhere quiet and private to weep. Her face suddenly felt so hot.

Dr. Burton continued speaking and now Wendy wished he would just stop and go away.

"You know, Wendy, post-lingual hearing loss isn't the end of the world. Your hearing aids will arrive soon; there will be some . . . adjustment to them. In the long term I suggest that you continue with your lip reading and signing classes."

What Dr. Burton was saying was that for Wendy to lose her hearing part-way through life, rather than at birth, wasn't so bad. She *knew* what sound was like – that was more than some people. How could he be so dry and matter-of-fact? Wendy thought, how could *he* – someone with perfect hearing – be the authority for those born without hearing – or losing their hearing at any time in their lives? To Dr. Burton, it was all just medical school jargon. But to Wendy, it was life-changing. He could never understand.

Wendy turned back towards the doctor as he was finishing his lecture. His wiry moustache seemed to bounce as he spoke, as if suspended on puppet strings. "It's just a matter of time until you lose your hearing completely." He cleared his throat as if trying to fill the silence that followed.

Momentarily the room felt suspended in time and then, as if sensing the worst possible moment, the receptionist poked her head through the door and shot an angry look at the doctor. "Mrs Lowry is waiting for you outside," she said, her sharp voice cutting through the silence, before curtly closing the door.

Wendy looked the doctor straight in the eye.

"I hear you loud and clear," she said, standing up from her seat. She didn't want to spend one more minute in this office. Dr. Burton raised a hand to stop her, but she promptly left the office with a stride in her step. She felt her dignity was worth more to her than being lectured by a man who clearly had no idea what life was like for any of his patients.

Wendy walked down the flagstone street of her town. Shop windows shone with spring displays, but she didn't care to look. Instead, as she walked, she listened to every single sound around her. She wrapped her green coat tightly around her. She felt sad, alone and like no one in the world understood her.

As Wendy walked along listening, she took in the sounds of birds chirping, a baby crying, and a woman letting out a loud laugh as she stood with a friend waiting for a bus . . . The bus engine rumbling down the road . . . A car's loud exhaust . . . The pedestrian crossing beeping, letting people know that it was safe to cross . . . All around her there were sounds with meaning, each sound carrying its own information.

The music from a car's stereo rang out from an open window, tinny and thin, but still it was *music*. Wendy loved music. It was a passion. She had a huge music collection spanning decades.

She loved pop music with its beats and catchy lyrics. She loved classical music, with the violins and brass, the grandeur and history. And rock music with its guitars and drums and then, on a day where she wanted some calm, she would turn to relaxing music, maybe with some pan flutes and even the intriguing sounds of dolphins and whales, suspended in a tranquil melody of synthesised strings.

Music moved and corralled her, like fine golden hands of gossamer reaching within her, massaging her emotions.

As she walked down the street she thought about her love of rhythm and beats and lyrics, her love for words and language, and the meaning it all gave.

She continued walking, not sure where she was going now, and came upon the local cinema, a place that she had, in the past, frequented as often as she could. She hadn't been there in some time lately. It was a 1930s stone building and she had walked past it on the hill in town so many times.

This time, she came to a halt in the street beside it. Her entire body became stationary in less than a second. A man walking along behind her nearly walked into her with his coffee.

"Be careful!" he called, bemused.

Wendy didn't care. She was focused on a brightly coloured poster outside the cinema now. It was for the old movie, *The Sound of Music*. The poster seemed to glow from the metal frame that held it, drawing her in. A banner at the bottom of the poster stated: "SPECIAL SCREENING – ONE DAY ONLY."

It appeared that the cinema was holding a special screening of the film at lunchtime. It was Wendy's favourite movie. She checked her watch. There was still ten minutes before the film would begin. Hastily, she walked into the cinema.

It was warm inside and everything seemed to be illuminated. The air was heavy with the smell of popcorn, and people milled around filling up bags with sweets – jelly snakes and coke bottles – and ordering large fizzy drinks. Popcorn glowed from large glass counters, and a girl in a red uniform and baseball cap smiled at her from behind the large shining red counter.

Wendy walked up to the girl behind the counter and asked for a ticket to the movie. The girl smiled and touched the screen in front of her, selecting the ticket.

"You can sit anywhere you like for this one. It's open seating." Wendy liked this – she could find a space away from people. The girl looked again at the screen in front of her, double checking something. "That'll be, eighteen . . ." The girl didn't finish her sentence and instead frowned. She looked very surprised at the price illuminated on her cash register screen.

Wendy saw that the girl was wearing a badge that said "TRAINEE." She was obviously very new and didn't know the movie prices yet. Wendy pulled the money from her purse and handed it to the girl, smiling.

"Oh, well, you *definitely* can't put a price on this!" Wendy said, cheerily.

The girl shrugged. "I don't know – it's still expensive," she said, looking at the ticket. She handed it to Wendy, still frowning at the price.

"Screen One," she said, turning to the next customer.

Wendy quickly found a seat four rows from the front where there was no one near her and sank down into the chair's soft red velvet, enjoying the private darkness of the cinema.

As the film began, she felt her heartbeat quicken as she thought, *When will I be able to hear Maria sing in a cinema again?*

She watched, entranced, as Maria, the heroine of the film, skipped through beautiful mountain pastures and sang her heart out. The music from the screen filled her mind. The high notes, the melodies and lyrics. She wanted to take it in, memorise it all, hold it forever. To have it on tap whenever she needed it.

For the future, for the darkest days, she wanted to know for absolute certain that she knew all the lyrics by heart. She wanted to know precisely what they sounded like and know how each song rose and fell.

She wanted the music to be accessible, like a rhythm inside her, under her skin. So that when she couldn't hear, she still could, in her mind. Her mind would be her jukebox and it wouldn't fail her.

She closed her eyes and listened, really listened, in a way that few ever listen. She captured notes and songs in her mind, like a camera capturing images. There, they would privately stay with her forever.

As one of the film's famous songs – "Do-Re-Mi" – began to play on the screen, Wendy sank down further into her cinema chair, the light from the screen illuminating her face.

She whispered along with the song:

> *Me, a name I call myself*
> *Far, a long, long way to run*
> *Sew, a needle pulling thread*
> *La, a note to follow Sew*
> *Tea, a drink with jam and bread…*

That was as far as Wendy could go. Her eyes were wide open and her lips trembled. She tried hard to fight the painful lump of emotion in her throat, because she was strong. She didn't cry. What good would it do? The screen filled her mind, and the colours began to blur as another song filled the theatre's walls.

It was finally here, in the darkness of the cinema, that she felt she had some peace. Hot silent tears ran down her cheeks and *The Sound of Music* filled her heart.

CHAPTER 8

Unwanted

W endy sat at home in her office designing a website for a unique shop specialising in unicorns. She moved the images of magical unicorns around on the screen, arranging them perfectly. They were all the colours of the rainbow and looked as though they could burst out from the screen. Wendy wished she had some magic in her life. She looked at her text phone and sighed. She had set it up and it sat on her desk, ready.

As she worked, she found herself thinking about Simon for a moment and wondering how he was. He seemed to be such a nice person.

She remembered the scrap of paper the girl at the animal shelter had given her. It was still in her coat pocket, but she hadn't touched it. She had looked at it in her car – it said "Simon direct phone" above the scrawled number. Now she realised that the odd girl had tried to get Wendy to call Simon directly.

She shook the thought of Simon from her head. *Why would he want to meet up with me?* she thought, overly critically. She didn't want him to know she was losing her hearing. She felt that he wouldn't be interested if he knew that. It was better just to avoid him.

But little did she know that Simon was in fact thinking about her too.

At the animal shelter, Simon stood at the front reception, ready to help anyone with their animal dilemmas. He was a trained vet tech and was studying to become a full veterinarian. In his spare time he liked to volunteer at the shelter and help to find the animals their forever homes.

There was no one at the reception desk for a moment, so Simon took his phone from his pocket and checked it for messages. There were none. He put his phone back in his pocket with a sigh. He had hoped that, after Sally had given Wendy his phone number, she would text him and he could find a way to make an introduction outside of the animal shelter.

He was getting ahead of himself, but he really wanted to see her again.

Just then, a woman started to try to push the reception door open with her back. It was clear that her hands were full with a cat basket. It was Wendy! Simon couldn't believe it. It was her same auburn hair and the same cat basket.

Simon ran to open the door for her as she backed her way into the reception.

"Hello again! I was just thinking about you!" he blurted out.

The woman turned around to face Simon. She looked shocked, furrowing her eyebrows. It wasn't Wendy at all! It was someone completely different – an older woman with big black glasses and a small Siamese cat.

Sally had walked into the reception and saw the whole thing. She stifled a laugh.

"Oh, I am so sorry!" Simon blushed. "I thought you were someone I – it doesn't matter. How can I help you?"

Sally raised an eyebrow at Simon as he walked back behind the counter. "Not your cat today?" she whispered to Simon, winking.

Simon shot Sally a sharp look and she scurried back through the employee door and out of the reception.

"I need your help," the woman began, thumping the cat basket onto the table in front of Simon.

A small creamy-coloured Siamese cat looked out from the basket, his blue eyes focusing on Simon as if to say, "Watch out!"

"I see," Simon said, pushing his glasses up his nose. He wasn't sure about the woman's tone of voice – she sounded angry and shook her head at him as she spoke.

"Listen, I'm not going to beat about the bush: it looks like an alien," the woman said, her large cheeks reddening. She extended her arm, bracelets along it jangling like a wind chime, and pointed a sausage-like finger at the small cat in an accusatory way. The cat looked out of the basket, blinking innocently.

"It's a beautiful Siamese cat, madam," Simon replied, shocked by the woman's mean comment about the gentle cat.

"Listen, I got it for my son. He laughed at it and said it looked like an alien with its face stretched out like that. He doesn't want it, so I'm bringing it back. Quite simple – I don't want any funny business."

"Funny business!" Simon shook his head. "I really think you need to –" As Simon was replying to the woman, the employee door banged open and Sally walked back into the reception, cutting him off mid-sentence.

"Oh no!" Sally cried as she rushed over to the basket "It's Mr. Bojangles!" she exclaimed. "What's wrong, is he OK?"

"He looks like an alien, that's what's wrong," the woman said, sharply glaring at Sally. "Are you going to give me my donation back or what? The boy doesn't want it."

Sally glared at the woman and took the cat basket from the table.

"You can go now," Sally said, holding the basket to her chest.

"Sally –" Simon tried to interject as the woman snatched at the basket.

"I paid good money for that; you can't just take it – I've got rights!"

"So does the cat!" Simon said now, his indignation at the woman's callous behaviour finally getting the better of him. "Donations aren't refundable. Consider it a good deed. All funds go to saving the lives of abused and unwanted animals – like this cat."

Simon and Sally now stood side by side staring at the woman and the cat let out a loud meow from his basket. The woman glared at them both. Clenching her fists, she stomped on the floor and Simon was almost certain he heard the woman snort. She was like a bull about to charge. She looked at Sally and then at the cat in the basket, before muttering to herself and finally leaving the reception. As the door slammed behind her Simon let out a loud sigh.

"Great, what are we going to do now? We're full!" Simon exclaimed, running a hand through his hair in exasperation. "What is happening this week? Apparently, no one wants to take responsibility for their cats!"

"Don't worry," Sally said, placing Mr. Bojangles gently back down on the table. "It's actually good – believe it or not. I have a friend who asked me about Mr. Bojangles a few days ago. She wanted to give him a home after she saw him on our website. She's finally ready to get a cat after she lost hers a few years ago and she really liked him. I told her he had found a home."

"Well, not anymore. Thank goodness," Simon said with a frown.

"Yes, thank goodness," Sally agreed, sticking her fingers through the basket where Mr. Bojangles rubbed his cheek gently against them. "He's such a sweetheart, I'll take him over to her tonight. Don't worry, everything has worked out for the best."

"But it doesn't always, does it?" Simon said, his thoughts far away. "I mean, that woman passed all of our adoption safety checks, and look what just happened. We're meant to be protecting animals, not delivering them into the hands of . . . who knows what." He trailed off in his thinking about the cat and started to think about Wendy. He was worried about her and worried about her cat. There was more to her story than she was letting on. He could tell.

CHAPTER 9

A Visitor

That evening, after finishing her work for the day, Wendy sat eating her dinner on her lap in front of the television. She was too tired to cook anything, so she had decided that a microwave meal would do.

Suddenly from the corner of her eye, Wendy noticed something outside her living room window. She turned her eyes from the TV and stared in disbelief. It was the cat!

"Go away!" Wendy shouted. She got up and walked towards the window with her fork still in her hand from her dinner. The cat looked through the glass at her, her green eyes unblinking.

Wendy banged on the glass with the side of her hand and the cat ran away, her tabby coat disappearing into the night like a ghost. Wendy stared out into the moonlit darkness of her garden. The moon was nearly full. Yet another month had passed since her grandmother had left them. Everything seemed to move so quickly these days. She sighed heavily. *What a strange cat*, she thought, feeling a little bit guilty about her reaction. She just didn't want the cat thinking it could stay around her house. As the time grew late,

Wendy switched off the TV and closed her eyes for a moment, covering herself with a blanket. She would go up to her bed soon.

The next morning Wendy awoke on the sofa. She hadn't bothered going to bed; she was too tired and ended up sleeping right where she was. As she became more awake, she could feel the strange sensation that someone was watching her. At first, she couldn't work out what it was.

She opened her eyes and gradually looked around the living room, then quickly her attention was turned to the living room window. The cat sat there, scratching at the glass, staring in at Wendy. Muddy paw prints were smeared all over the glass.

Wendy sat up sharply, her hair all around her face in a mess. She looked at the cat and, enraged, she pulled off one of her slippers and hurled it at the window.

"Get lost!" she shouted.

As the slipper hit the window, it bounced and the cat leapt away, her legs almost a blur as her body flew like a rocket away from the window. The slipper ricocheted back from the window, directly towards a side table next to Wendy's TV.

The slipper smacked against the side table, knocking its thin wooden legs and sending it rocking. On top of the table sat the pretty vase Wendy had collected from her grandmother's house.

The vase spun, turned, rocked, and, before Wendy could stop it, hit the floor with a loud smash!

"No!" Wendy cried out. She shook her head in despair. This was terrible. That was the vase that Grandma had left for Wendy as a gift. It had been so beautiful – its white porcelain was so delicate and it was painted with a beautiful deep blue that swirled around the vase like ocean waves.

Now it lay on the floor, smashed into many pieces. Large, sharp triangles of porcelain and tiny fragmented pieces were scattered, all mixed together on the carpet. Wendy bent down to carefully pick up the pieces and to see if there was anything she could do to save the vase. It looked unfixable.

As she knelt, she noticed the corner of an envelope sticking out from underneath a large piece of the broken vase. She frowned, wondering what it could be underneath the porcelain. She carefully moved the piece with her fingertips, making sure not to cut her fingers. As she lifted the shard, a small, white, crinkled envelope was revealed. Wendy breathed in. How did it get there?

Then she remembered: the removal man must have accidentally dropped it inside the vase. She had been calling her father at the time and had forgotten all about it.

She picked up the envelope and blew dust from the broken porcelain from it. Carefully, with shaking hands, she opened its sealed edge.

Inside the envelope a pretty note card peeked out. Wendy pulled it out and held it in front of her. It was a beautiful image of a garden, full of roses blooming. There were red roses, pink roses, white and yellow, even magenta. The sky was blue and small swallows flew side by side. Some of the roses were outlined with shining gold ink – Wendy smiled at its beauty.

She opened the card, almost holding her breath. She wasn't sure what it could say or why Grandma had written to her.

Wendy began to read the rickety writing. Grandma must have somehow gathered the strength to write it while she was unwell. This made Wendy's heart ache.

> *Wendy, please let go of the idea that losing your hearing is going to ruin your life. What will ruin your life is your attitude. You lose some things – but in life you will also discover some new things, wonderful things.*
>
> *Even if you are going to hear less, you may find that you are going to see a lot more – I hope so!*
>
> *All my love forever, Grandma xxx*

Wendy wiped a tear from her cheek as it rolled. Her eyes became blurry and her throat felt tight and hurt. A big ball of emotion felt like it was rolling up her throat from her heart. She rubbed over her heart with her hand; it hurt thinking about her dear grandma. She missed her so much.

She realised that her grandma had been worried about her before she passed away. Grandma wanted Wendy to realise that she was no different from anyone else and that losing her hearing did not mean that she had to hide away in her work. Grandma painted a picture for Wendy, and somehow her thoughts seemed clear for a moment.

Grandma had wanted her to understand that the things that count in life are inside of us. How we love, how we care, how we talk to ourselves in our heads and how we speak to our friends and family.

She wanted Wendy to know that even if she were losing her hearing, she would find herself – her own sense of inner strength.

"The things in life that matter cannot be bought," her grandma had always said. She was right.

It was likely that because Wendy was losing her hearing partway through her life, that when she lip-read and had conversations with people, they would have no idea that she could not hear them. People would not realise how much hard work and how many adjustments Wendy had made in her life. She thought to herself about that achievement.

She breathed in deeply and let out a sigh. She had a long road ahead of her. And she still felt very unsure of herself, but Grandma's words brought a moment of calm and clear reflection to Wendy for the first time in many months.

Later that day, Wendy sat working in her office. She was working on a website for a jewellery brand called Toliso Jewels and was placing images of different necklaces and bracelets into different arrangements on the screen.

Just then, Wendy's new phone lit up. The screen flashed, letting her know that a call from Bryan was incoming. His name flashed up on the screen and Wendy rolled her eyes; she knew that he would be shouting into the phone the way he always did. She hunched her shoulders, ready for his loud voice, and lifted the phone's receiver.

"Hello, Wendy! Do you hear me? Are you using your new phone? Over!" His voice yelled from the speaker as he shouted into the phone. For some strange reason, he was communicating as though he was using a walkie-talkie.

"Do you have the installation software for the business use Web-Designer 9000? Over!" he continued, still shouting.

It must make his throat sore, Wendy thought.

"OK, Bryan, we got the phone so that you don't have to strain. I'll have a look for the software – I can send it to you."

Wendy smiled at her own joke. She wanted Bryan to get the message that he didn't need to treat the phone as though it were a loudspeaker at the fairgrounds.

Looking at her new phone, she could see that everything said in conversation was repeated on the screen in text, right there for her to read. At least the phone worked well.

Wendy poked her head under her desk to see if the pen drive containing the software was in a small box she kept under there. The box had all kinds of stationery in it – so, she reasoned, that could be where she placed the pen drive after she had installed the software on her computer. Bryan had obviously lost his copy.

As she rummaged through the stationery box, she noticed the box that she had brought home from Grandma's house sitting next to it. She had been meaning to go through it but she knew that it would be painful – looking through Grandma's treasured things. She had put the box there just to keep her office tidy and to keep these items safe until she felt ready to deal with the emotions that would surface by looking through them.

She took the box out from under her desk and looked inside it. A silver frame caught her eye and she pulled it from the box. It was a photo of her together with Grandma. Wendy must have been about ten in the photo. She and her grandma were smiling, wearing aprons with hearts on them. They had been baking together in the kitchen at Grandma's cottage.

Wendy remembered that day with a sigh. It had been the summer holidays from school and Grandma was teaching Wendy how to make a tasty summer strawberry flan. They had eaten more straw-berries than they had ended up baking, but it didn't matter. The main thing was they had fun together.

Wendy placed the photo on top of her desk, smiling at the memory.

Wendy sat with a cup of her favourite strawberry tea on the red sofa in her living room; the cup was warm and comforting in her hands. She thought about her phone call with Bryan – he had been utterly eccentric – as usual. He had actually blown that stupid whistle of his down the phone when she had finally found the pen drive – and then asked her what the phone screen said. *Next time I see him,* she thought, *if he does that again, I'm going to take that whistle and –* something caught the corner of her eye, distracting her, and she looked out of the window but there was nothing there. She shrugged and sipped her tea – she thought about listening to some music on her MP3 player, but the idea made her feel depressed as she wouldn't be able to hear every sound like she used to. She paused for a moment and then decided to put the headphones over her ears anyway.

She could still hear the music – the beats and the low notes – but the high notes and the more delicate instrumentals were becoming lost. She loved music; for Wendy, the intricacy of a song was like reading a book. Music told a story, and every note could evoke a scene or emotion. High notes were happy; there were chimes that could make a person feel as though they were in a crisp, icy cold place like Scandinavia, and drums that could make a person feel that they were walking the plains of Africa. Futuristic sounds and classical sounds. There were so many stories music could tell, and she didn't want to lose that world of pure enjoyment, landscapes, storyscapes and wonder.

She began to cry, thinking about a future which wasn't here yet – a bleak future, which seemed to be moving ever closer to her. It wasn't fair. Why was she being forced to be strong? Why did she have to face this challenge?

Grandma had always told Wendy that challenges in life make up part of who we are. They make us stronger. And if we didn't have challenges, how could we appreciate the good times, if we had nothing that wasn't so good to compare them to? If we just went through life in a perfect dream, perhaps we would never feel deep and true appreciation for the magic of a beautiful day in the sunshine or a fun day out with friends, our favourite dinner or a lovely surprise. There was always something to be grateful for.

Wendy tried to remember Grandma's words as she cried. She knew it was important. She took a tissue from a box beside the sofa and blew her nose. She breathed in deeply, feeling the strength inside her.

She wanted to travel more, to see the world and one day help other people who were in a similar situation of losing their hearing. She wanted to use her skills with computers and the internet to help bring together people from all over the world who were hard of hearing, deaf, and experiencing their own journeys with hearing loss.

She felt a sense of resolve come over her. She still felt tired from crying and decided that it would be a good time to make herself another nice warm cup of tea.

As Wendy got up, something at the window caught her eye again. It was the cat – looking sad as she gazed in through the window. Her coat was beginning to get wet as light rain started to fall outside. Wendy felt a change inside of her. Suddenly she wasn't thinking about how she felt anymore; she was wondering how *the cat* was feeling – she felt compassion for the cat. All through her childhood she had disliked cats because her parents had paraded them in front of her and it had made her feel second best. But now, this cat was looking for a friend. How could Wendy hope for people to understand her when she wasn't trying to understand this cat?

"Empathy," Wendy said out loud to herself. "That's what the world needs. More empathy."

Wendy walked towards the window and the cat looked up at her longingly. Her brown tabby coat was beginning to look almost black as the rain soaked it through, and her green eyes shone through the dim light, as though alight from within. She looked into Wendy's eyes and Wendy looked back at her, really looked at her now, and saw the cat's delicate face looking back, hoping to make friends. She noticed, for the first time, the cat's white whiskers, her little pink nose, and the green collar that Grandma had given her.

Wendy opened the living room window and the cat walked in, carefully balancing on the windowsill with her small paws. Wendy quickly closed the window behind the cat, making sure not to let the rain in.

"Wait there," Wendy said as she went to fetch a small hand towel from the bathroom. She returned and began to gently dry the cat's coat. Her fur stood up on end as Wendy dried it with the towel; it made the cat look like a big porcupine.

"There you go, that's better," Wendy said, and the cat jumped down onto the carpet and gave her fur a quick shake. She was nearly dry now and her fur looked fluffy from its rub-down with the towel.

Wendy sat down on the sofa – she felt tired. The cat wandered over to the sofa and brushed against Wendy's shin. Wendy didn't move; she still felt a bit awkward with the cat. The cat let out a small trill that sounded like a high-pitched "Brrr!" sound. Then she jumped onto the sofa next to Wendy. She placed a paw delicately on Wendy's leg, testing to see whether Wendy would move. Then, she placed her other front paw on Wendy's leg. Then, all of a sudden, she was trying to sit on Wendy's lap! She moved around in a circle trying to get comfortable, her tail waving in Wendy's face.

"No, thank you!" Wendy said in response to this.

She gently moved the cat from her lap and onto the sofa next to her.

"Don't get used to it. You can't stay for long, I really don't have room in my life for a cat."

The cat looked at Wendy with her green Cleopatra eyes, as if understanding, and Wendy felt a little guilty. But nonetheless, she really couldn't handle any more in her life. She felt like she had enough to cope with already – *without* the addition of a cat.

The cat curled herself into a neat ball against a fluffy cushion and closed her eyes, letting out a small sigh.

Wendy looked at the cat with her brown tabby coat and her tail with its distinctive black tip. Her eyes were framed with black markings like the ancient Egyptian queen, Cleopatra. The top of her head sported markings in the shape of an M. She was a true tabby cat. With her regal grace and refined features, she looked like the type of cat you could imagine seeing in ancient Egyptian times.

Wendy remembered a book she had once read on ancient Egypt. The book had a chapter on cats in ancient Egyptian society, and Wendy recalled that the book had said that cats were considered to be like gods in Egypt – they were even worshipped. If anyone killed a cat, they would lose their lives – that was the law. What would they make of her ignoring this cat?

It was an odd thought and Wendy shook it away from her mind. She had bigger things to think about. She felt confused and lonely, and wondered when, if ever, she would stop feeling this way.

"Oh, Grandma," Wendy whispered to herself, "why aren't you here?"

CHAPTER 10

Never Alone

That night, Wendy sat upright in her bed reading, and the little cat sat by her bedroom door, neatly curled into an oval shape, her head resting on her paws. Wendy was reading the diary of a young woman who traveled on a solo trip by motorcycle through South America. She loved the idea of taking off into the sunset and feeling free as a bird.

She turned the page in her book and came to a photo of Cartagena, a beautiful city in Colombia: white buildings surrounded a public square and a small child walked with his mother who carried brightly coloured scarves to a nearby market. It was a place that Wendy would like to see one day.

Wendy suddenly remembered the time that she and Grandma had taken a trip to see a travelling circus of acrobats and contortionists from France. It had been wonderful to see the performers' sparkling costumes and watch them fly through the air on trapezes as silk streamed behind them like wings. She and Grandma had also seen contortionists who could miraculously twist their entire bodies into small boxes on the stage; it was as though they were made from rubber!

They had planned – Grandma and Wendy – to take a trip together one day to see this circus group perform in their hometown of Paris. It was a happy memory and Wendy felt sad that she wouldn't get the chance to live their dream to travel to Paris together.

She had placed the book she was reading face down on her lap now and she felt sad. As she sat thinking about her grandmother, a cool breeze blew in through Wendy's bedroom window. It was only open a fraction but it was enough to make Wendy shudder.

She put the book on the table beside her bed and looked at her old Moroccan-style bedside lamp, a gift from Grandma. She had always liked that lamp; the small holes that were cut in its metal frame scattered light all around her bedroom. It made the light look like golden stars dotted about the walls. She switched it off and settled back into her bed. "Night," she called to the cat, who replied with a small chirping sound, as though she understood.

She pulled the blankets up to her ears as the breeze drifted into the room again and rustled her white curtains as it made its entrance. The room wasn't completely dark – bright white light shone from the moon outside, through a gap in the curtains, casting shadows onto her bedroom wall.

She watched the bedroom wall in front of her as shadow branches from the large beech tree outside her house silhouetted in black against it. The fine long shadows of the branches bounced up and down on the wall in the moonlight, as though animated in conversation with one another. They moved and swayed, their spindly shadows energised as they were corralled by the breeze outside.

As Wendy lay watching the shadows, they seemed to shift and change. Left, then right, they moved, up, then down. They seemed to be maneuvering themselves about the wall.

Wendy blinked her eyes. The shadows were definitely changing. As she continued watching them with intense curiosity, she could feel her heart quicken. She barely dared to breathe, as the shadows moved faster and faster. In the shadowy moonlight, she swore that she could see the face of her grandmother appearing on the wall.

As the branches finally stopped moving, there on the wall was the profile of her grandmother's face. The branches had woven together to create her exact image – Wendy was sure of it. There was no mistaking Grandma's round soft chin, her smiling mouth, her strong but small nose and her curly hair, tumbling about her shoulders.

Wendy smiled, looking at the shadow. She didn't feel scared; somehow it felt completely normal. She remembered Grandma's thick red hair and its sweet vanilla scent as she hugged her. Her soft warm hugs radiated love. Suddenly, Wendy felt very calm and sleepy; a deep sense of reassurance filled her and her eyes began to close. She forced them open, resisting the urge to sleep and focused on the wall where the shadows sat. Now, all that she saw was the scraggly shadow of the branches, just as they were before; Grandma's face was gone.

Soon, Wendy was fast asleep – she couldn't fight the sensation that filled her. She needed to rest and recuperate. It was a clear, starry night outside and the moon was so bright that, even without streetlights, a person could easily see where they were walking.

The night was calm and silent and, outside the window, small bats chased through the night air catching insects. An owl hooted in the distance, the beech trees beside the road moved gently in the breeze – and Wendy, all the while, slept quietly in her cozy bed with the covers tucked up around her.

Wendy never heard the glass break in her front door, nor the crow bar breaking the wood. She never heard the front door banging open, nor the glass crunching under the burglar's feet as he stepped into her house. She was still fast asleep.

CHAPTER 11

A True Friend

Now that the burglar had broken into Wendy's house, he stood in the doorway, deciding where to go first. He looked down the hallway. Then he walked fast towards the living room.

The burglar was dressed in a dark blue hoodie and wore a black baseball cap beneath the hood so that people wouldn't see his face. He wore leather gloves and carried a large bag with a crow bar inside it. He was like a demon in the night and upstairs, Wendy was in terrible danger.

Another person in the same situation might have heard the intrusion, but all was silent to Wendy. Even worse was the fact that she was all alone and had no one to help her.

The burglar looked around. He saw the newish TV in the living room and a laptop sitting on the sofa, and he smiled to himself. He noticed a photo in the living room of a girl and an old lady. This place was easy pickings. It likely belonged to some frail old lady, he thought. He would take what he wanted and no one could stop him. He rubbed his leather-gloved hands together, happy with himself.

He turned around and placed a booted foot on the first step of the staircase. Then, the second step. He was going to see what was upstairs. He wasn't scared – he had his crow bar. If anyone got in his way, he would deal with them.

Just then, he heard a noise in the living room. The sound of something clattering to the floor cut through the silence. He turned sharply from the staircase and looked towards the living room. He stepped down the stairs, his boots thudding, and backed into the silent darkness of the living room. On the floor lay the photo of the girl and the old lady. It had been on a table by the TV.

He shrugged – it was nothing. He turned back towards the staircase hastily and placed his big boot on the first stair.

Suddenly, he was knocked in the back of the head from behind. He lost his balance and lunged forward onto the stairs, putting his hands out in front of him as he fell. Something large and soft had hit him.

"What the . . ." he exclaimed into the darkness, rubbing the back of his head.

Before he could finish his sentence, he felt a sharp pain in his leg.

"Ouch!" he cried.

He shook his leg hard and turned around, grabbing at his leg. There was nothing there. It must be a dog. He raised his crowbar into the air like a baseball bat, ready to attack. He looked into the darkness, squinting, expecting to see the snarling jaws of a dog – a Doberman or Alsatian. He could hear his own breathing in the silence of the night.

A small silhouette moved on the floor in front of him and his beady eyes focused on it. The dark blue, black shape came into focus. A small cat looked up at him and now he began to laugh.

His angry face was caught by the moonlight as it shone through the open front door, half revealing his gnarled, mean features, and he grimaced in a horrible expression at the little cat.

"Silly little kitty," he said, drawing the crow bar up into the air. He would get rid of this nuisance of a cat. It had bitten him and jumped at him. Now he would teach it a lesson, he thought.

The cat wasn't about to wait to see what the man was going to do. She gathered her strength and bounded off of the floor as though springing from a trampoline. She flew through the air towards the burglar, her claws outstretched, and landed straight on his head. She knew that he was a very dangerous person. But she had to do something to stop him!

The burglar turned this way and that, yelling. He fell heavily to the ground next to the front door, but still she would not let go of his head. She dug her claws into him as though he was a big pin cushion. He pulled at her with his large gloved hands, but this just made his situation worse. She hissed and growled and her fur stood on end. Her tail was twice its normal size, fluffed up and bushy like a big pine tree, as she blazed with rage at him, her eyes glowing like molten embers in the moonlight.

He cried like a baby and tried to get up from the floor and pull her from his head, but she just clawed even more. He knocked into a side table by the front door, sending it flying, and even though this scared her, she would not let go. She knew she had to get him out of the house and away from Wendy.

Finally, with the cat still on his head, the burglar fled down the garden pathway and out towards the street. It was his only option.

He sobbed as he ran and tried not to scream because he didn't want anyone to call the police. Once he had made it onto the street, the cat let go of his head and sprang on her nimble legs up into a tree and into the leafy safety of its branches, far away from the evil burglar. He staggered down the street, still grasping at his head, his baseball cap nowhere to be seen.

She clambered high up into the leafy tree until she found a sturdy branch to rest upon. She looked down at the pretty street. Catching her breath, she could see that the full moon illuminated the houses, and all was still. It didn't seem like it was possible for such awful things to happen on this street.

The cat watched Wendy's front door moving idly in the breeze, smashed open by the burglar. Her green eyes caught the light of a passing car and mirrored it back, glowing like golden orbs floating in the darkness. The driver looked up, startled as he passed.

She surveyed the street, sitting motionless upon the branch, like a statue of a cherub carved onto the side of a church in sandstone.

The evening breeze drifted through the tree, rustling its silky leaves. The air was cold against her fur and she wrapped her brown-and-black-striped tail tightly around her like a scarf. She sat steadfast on the branch, monitoring everything, making sure that the burglar did not return to Wendy's home.

As she sat and watched Wendy's door, it wasn't long until she heard the sound of glass breaking farther up the street. It resounded in her sensitive cat ears and she twitched them, like satellite dishes focusing them towards the sound. She heard the exact direction it came from and could pinpoint where it was happening.

She turned her head sharply and looked up the street, rising from her sitting position on the branch. She stretched her legs, arched her back and yawned – she was tired now. Then she began to climb carefully down the tree back towards the pavement.

CHAPTER 12

Saved

Wendy felt a soft warm pressure on her chest as she drifted away from her dream. Dreamy images and colours faded into white light as she awoke and opened her eyes. At first blink all she saw was a blur. She felt something cold touch her nose. She closed her eyes, thinking she was dreaming. There it was again. Something furry prodded her cheek. She blinked her eyes open again and this time she saw a large pair of round green eyes staring back into her own.

"Aghh!" she cried in surprise.

She rolled and the heaviness left her chest. It was the cat! She had been sitting on Wendy's chest and had prodded her face with her paw to wake her up.

Wendy was just about to scold the cat when she looked at the clock next to her bed. It was flashing "9:00 a.m." Wendy was meant to have awoken at 8:00 this morning; she was now an hour late!

She sat up in bed, flustered. She had missed her alarm, again. She hadn't heard it at all! If the cat hadn't woken Wendy – she would have missed her class entirely! Wendy had sign language class at 9:30

that morning and now she really needed to rush. It was a twenty-minute drive to the class. She would have to skip breakfast.

Wendy chased down the stairs with her wet hair flying behind her; she didn't have time to dry it. A quick shower was all she could do in the time. As she stepped from the last stair and into the hallway that led to the front door, she looked down, rummaging in her purse for her car key.

She did not notice the small cat, sitting beside the overturned table at the end of the hallway, until she looked up from her bag, her car key in hand. Immediately her face fell.

She walked slowly in disbelief towards the overturned table, and then to the front door. Broken glass lay scattered on the floor and the door bumped loosely against the doorframe in the wind.

Even the wooden doorframe was damaged, splintered and broken where the crow bar had been forced against it. The glass panel in the door had been smashed and there were dirty boot prints leading along the hallway. Everything was a mess.

Wendy's heart pounded as she thought about her laptop for work and her other possessions. She ran back along the hallway to check the living room. She held her breath with worry as she looked into the room. She couldn't believe it – it was untouched! She let out a sigh. The small carriage clock ticked on the mantlepiece, beating out the seconds as though nothing had happened. The TV was still there and her laptop was on the sofa where she had left it.

"I can't believe it!" she said aloud to herself. She turned to look at the cat, who was sitting calmly in the hallway, cleaning her face with a paw.

Wendy was bewildered and in shock at what she had discovered this morning.

"What do you think happened?" Wendy asked the cat. She obviously didn't expect a reply, but she didn't expect what the cat did next either. Suddenly, without warning, the cat's ears twitched forward as though she had heard something, and she took off out of the front door, her legs propelling her like a little rocket, as usual.

"Where are you going now?"

Wendy called after her, but it was no use; the cat was gone. The cat raced on her four small tabby cat legs as though she had somewhere very important to be. Wendy couldn't understand why she would just disappear like that – especially at a time like this.

Wendy closed her eyes and sighed again, looking back at the hallway behind her – the overturned table, the glass, the boot prints and the mess. It was horrible. As she looked at the scene, she tried to piece together what might have happened. She focused clearly on the hallway now and something caught her eye. Beside the overturned table, on the floor, lay a black baseball cap. Wendy crouched down, looking at the cap – it was torn and shredded. *How did the cap get like that?* she wondered – it was very odd.

She kicked the hat with her toe. She was angry at the vile burglar for damaging her home. As she kicked the hat, it skidded across the floor and into the overturned table, which lay on its side. She stepped over to the table and lifted it back up into its correct position against the wall. As she did, she noticed a green velvet cat collar beneath the edge of the table.

Wendy picked up the collar and held it in her hand. She looked down at the cap on the floor again. It really did look like it had been put through a shredder. She shook her head in disbelief. Was it possible that the cat had defended her last night?

She held the soft collar in her hand and thought for a moment about the cat, and the burglary – and what could have happened. She realised that she needed to call the police.

She pulled her phone from her pocket and dialed a number on the screen.

"Hello, police . . ." She would need to give them as much information as possible. Suddenly Wendy felt like she needed to sit down – she realised that she had been very, very lucky.

That night Wendy watched television absent-mindedly. She wasn't really paying attention to anything on the screen – there was too much on her mind.

It had been a long and expensive day. First Wendy had to get the front door fixed – and it wasn't easy to find someone who could fix the door right away. Then Wendy had to catch up on her work and let her sign language tutor know why she hadn't made it to her class. At the end of the day, she still hadn't quite caught up on all her work.

As the sun set and it began to grow dark, the door was finally fixed and Wendy felt safe in her own home once more.

After all of the stress and hassle, Wendy decided that she wanted something tasty for dinner and so she decided to make her favourite dinner – spaghetti with pesto. Unfortunately, in the end she couldn't eat much at all. She stared at the TV screen, her thoughts elsewhere, and pushed the spaghetti around on her plate.

She was worried; it was 7:30 in the evening and there was no sign of the cat. Usually by now, she would have come to the window. But there was nothing. As the evening rolled on and the carriage clock hands moved around to ten in the evening, still there was no sign of the cat.

Wendy flicked channels on her television and let the channel sit on the ten o'clock news. She wasn't the biggest fan of the news because she didn't like to hear all the negativity. But she did like to watch a new segment they had introduced to the news about travel.

It was only a ten-minute show, but each day they would have a presenter informing the viewers about things to see and do while visiting a different city around the world – and she wanted to see where they were going to be this week. She hoped it would take her mind off the cat's disappearance.

She got up and went into the kitchen to make herself some hot chocolate; she felt like having something sweet. As she made the chocolate, she reasoned that she was probably worrying needlessly about the cat – and that the cat would return to her window sometime soon, whenever she wanted to. *Yes, that's it*, she told herself. *By tomorrow she'll be sitting here with me again and I can thank her. I will have gone to my sign language class and everything will be back to normal.* She reassured herself with these thoughts as she stirred her chocolate and walked back into the living room.

She sat back on the sofa and picked up her laptop, looking over a web design for a whale watching company. It had been a very enjoyable work project. The images were fantastic, featuring dolphins and whales moving through the beautiful blue ocean. She enjoyed everything involved in creating a website that was to promote seeing these beautiful animals in their natural environment, gliding through the deep blue sea.

She tried to finish the design, but she kept making mistakes as her mind was still on the cat. She was closing her laptop when, suddenly, voices coming from the TV screen seemed to grow louder with excitement, grabbing her attention.

A man's voice was speaking rapidly on the news and Wendy was sure she heard him say something about a cat, just a moment ago.

She scrunched up her nose – surely not! Putting her laptop down, she turned up the volume.

On the screen a middle-aged man and a vivacious woman spoke in animated voices, their faces smiling and excited.

"I just don't know Louise – a cat, can you believe it?" the man said, gesturing with his hands in disbelief.

"That is what the couple said, Aaron, a cat. She stepped right in and saved them. When the police arrived this morning she was nearby. But when an officer attempted to approach her – she apparently 'evaded' him. Those were his words."

The newsreader laughed and Wendy grimaced at the screen. She got up and stood in front of the TV now, her hands on her hips. The newsreader continued, shimmying excitedly in her seat.

"This really is local news at its best. You've heard of cat burglars but never cat bodyguards."

The newsreaders laughed in high-pitched bursts together, throwing their heads back as though this was the funniest joke they had ever heard. The male newsreader arched an eyebrow and looked into the camera.

"The couple says that she did the job of two guard dogs in chasing the burglar away from their home. Good job, kitty! Now, as they are elderly, they were checked into hospital this morning with shock, but they have been given a full bill of health and are said to be offering a reward."

"A reward?" the lady newsreader repeated, raising her eyebrows and turning to face the camera with false surprise.

"A reward?" Wendy said out loud. This sounded like bad news. Now everyone would be out looking for the cat, or pretending their cat had helped the couple. The newsreaders continued their chatter.

"Yes, Louise, if anyone knows the whereabouts of the cat. Described as a small tabby cat with green eyes – that's all we have to go on. If this is *your* cat, please let us know at the following number . . .”

Wendy flicked the television off with the remote. She had heard enough. She couldn't believe it! That must have been where the cat had rushed off to this morning – she had wanted to check on those people. She had not only saved Wendy but she had saved the elderly couple on her street!

It was too late to call Mrs Budnick now. She would definitely be asleep and Wendy didn't want to alarm her. Wendy would make sure to speak to her, first thing tomorrow. She wanted to check that Mrs Budnick was OK.

She also wanted to say thank you to the cat and make sure that *she* was unharmed after everything that had happened. Wendy was very grateful to the little cat for her heroic acts of protection. She just hoped that the cat would be safe. Wendy felt nervous as she thought about the little cat out there, all alone. Some people might want to pretend that she was their cat, so that they could claim the reward and take her away. She shook her head – the little cat wasn't safe.

Wendy felt a horrible worry as she thought about what could happen. She stared at the window where the cat would normally visit, and gulped, her heart now racing.

CHAPTER 13

The Search Begins

It was a blustery overcast day – Spring seemed to have disappeared. Leaves fell from the trees outside in twirling spirals down to the ground, and rain pattered on the roof. Wendy had decided to work from the living room so that she could keep an eye out for the cat at the window. She had to work on a website for a travel company.

The travel company was advertising guided tours in different cities around the world. It was a novel and exciting idea and Wendy was desperate to travel, but today it didn't interest her at all.

Normally she would have really enjoyed this kind of project, but she was tired and worried because there was still no sign of the cat. She had barely slept that night, thinking about what could happen to the little cat at the hands of people who just wanted her for their own gain.

She had called Mrs Budnick at least six times and left two messages. At lunchtime she had even knocked on her door, but there was no answer.

Wendy looked up at the window to see if the cat was there, her eyes scanning her garden for any sign of movement. It must have been the hundredth time in less than two hours that she had looked to see if the cat had appeared. She couldn't stand it anymore. She got up from her work and walked over to the window, standing so close to the glass that her breath misted it up.

"Where are you?" she said out loud, frustrated and worried. "Why won't you come back?"

That was *it*; she couldn't take it any longer! She stood up, slipped on her shoes and picked up her door keys from the side table in the hallway. Hastily, she made her way out the front door and up the street.

She walked up the neat pathway to Mrs Budnick's front door again and knocked hard. She knocked on the door so hard that she even made the stained glass rattle in its frame above the door. She stood and waited. And knocked again. There was silence; no one came to the door.

"Come on!" she cried out, stomping her feet in frustration. That was it! She couldn't stand not knowing where the cat was. She would continue her search and she would find the cat herself. She was sure to bring her home, she reasoned.

Wendy looked under hedges and even up in the trees. At one point she stood under one of the large beech trees outside her home and called up at the tree.

"If you're up there, please come down," she said, shaking a small bag of cat biscuits that she had bought for the cat.

A woman with a baby in a pram saw Wendy calling up at the tree and crossed the street with a worried expression on her face. Wendy didn't care. If she had to, she would call for the cat in the middle of an arena filled with thousands of people staring at her.

Wendy walked all the way to the end of her street; she peered over garden walls and even climbed a fence to glimpse into a garden to see if perhaps the cat was there. She even had two small poodles chase her from one front garden when she made the mistake of opening the gate and walking down the garden path uninvited.

She crossed the street and walked past houses and apartments, looking to see if the cat was somewhere on the opposite side of the street. She even looked down a drain cover. She realised that this was a desperate move, but her mind was wandering, turning to all kinds of different scenarios.

What if the cat has been stolen by someone who wanted it for the reward? What if the cat fell down somewhere and was trapped? she thought. These thoughts kept spinning and whirling in her mind like a tornado picking up speed.

She went to the small local grocer's and bought a bar of her favourite chocolate: *Miss Mabel's Finest Chocolate* – the silver wrapper shone and Wendy unwrapped it eagerly, taking a large bite. She felt stressed and craved something sweet. The hours of worry were making her feel tired.

She was about to leave the store when she decided to ask the shopkeeper whether he had seen or heard anything about a small tabby cat with green eyes. He rubbed his grey beard and scratched his head thinking about it. Finally he said that he hadn't.

Then, just as she was walking out through the door, he scratched his head again and called out to her.

"Hang on!"

Wendy turned around eagerly.

"There was a young man in here earlier asking me if I sell cat bags – you know – to carry a cat in if it goes somewhere. A travel bag."

Wendy turned. "Oh really?" She thought for a second. "What did he look like?"

"Well, he was big, with dark hair, and well, I don't think I've seen him around here before." He shrugged.

Wendy looked at him expectantly, as though he held the key to a great mystery.

"Anyway, I don't sell cat bags so he left," he continued, turning to the next customer at the till and scanning a magazine that the customer had put in front of him. "That's about it though on the topic of cats. Sorry, love." He smiled apologetically.

Wendy's face dropped. "No, no problem." She forced a smile. As she walked out of the shop, she was unsure of what to do next and slightly worried that there was a strange man in the vicinity looking to buy a bag to transport a cat.

Could it be related? She wasn't sure, but her stomach churned with anxiety. What if he had seen the story on the news and was a crazy man looking to exploit the cat to make money? Or a scientist who wanted to trap the cat because of her extraordinary intelligence?

She had to push the thoughts from her mind. It was too much to bear. Walking home she felt thoroughly defeated as she had visualised seeing the cat on the path and carrying her home, but it didn't happen.

The clouds moved in as she walked back down the street and the beech trees rustled as the wind picked up. Spring showers loomed heavy in the sky as the clouds grew a dirty grey with rain.

As Wendy reached her front door, large drops of rain began to fall slowly, making their arrival known as they patted loudly against the ground. They hit the green jacket she was wearing with a smacking sound as she searched for her door key in her bag. She made it indoors just in time as the sky opened up and the rain fell in a deluge.

Wendy hung up her coat on a peg in the hallway and made a beeline for the kitchen. She put the kettle on to boil and then made her way upstairs to her office.

She knelt and reached under her desk for the cardboard box that she had collected from Grandma's house the day that her furniture was being moved. Inside the box sat a white china teapot. It had been Grandma's for many years and dated back to the Victorian era. It had belonged to Grandma's mother and it was very precious. It was over one hundred years old.

Wendy picked it up out of the box carefully and looked at its fine white porcelain. It was round like a cherry, with golden flowers hand painted around the top near the lid.

Carefully, she carried the tea pot down the stairs, minding each step – she didn't want to slip. Her socks were a little bit slippery against the carpet and she resisted the urge to walk at a faster pace.

She took the teapot into the kitchen and carefully washed it before lifting the dainty porcelain lid. She would make her favourite tea – strawberry – and think about what she was going to do to find the cat.

As she drank her tea, she sat back on her sofa and stared out of the window where the cat would usually come and look in at her. Despondently, she slumped back and then suddenly she heard the thud of something falling to the ground.

"Drat," she said, straining under the sofa to reach whatever it was that had fallen to the floor.

Reaching under the sofa, she pulled out a book – it was her sign language book. She looked at it, then remembered: she had sign language class – they had an important evaluation this evening!

She looked at the carriage clock opposite; it was 5:30 already – and class started in 15 minutes in town! She needed to get a move on. If she was late for any more classes, they might not allow her to continue with the course. She didn't have a second to spare.

CHAPTER 14

A Forgotten Promise

Wendy's sign language class was crowded this evening. Their usual classroom at the community college had been taken up by a group of adults who were trying to play musical instruments of various kinds. As a result, Wendy's sign language class had been moved into a much smaller classroom. There weren't enough chairs for everybody, so some people had to sit on the floor. Luckily for Wendy, the disruption had delayed the start of the class and no one made a fuss about her late arrival – in fact, no one really noticed.

The other class – which had forced them from their usual room – was some kind of New Age 'musical appreciation' class where adults got together and attempted to play basic musical instruments, in a very shambolic way, running around a bit like when they were five-year-olds at school.

The New Age group might have had good intentions, but clearly they had no musical experience – they really didn't have a clue what they were doing. For anyone looking on at the class, it was a very odd sight: grown men and women standing, holding brightly coloured kazoos, blowing down them as hard as they could while duck-like squawks blasted from their instruments, filling the room with all kinds of jarring sounds.

Wendy sat at a desk opposite her sign language partner. Before they began practice, the instructor made apologies for the change of room. They would try freestyle signing with their partner before going on to study new words and phrases later on, followed by an evaluation. As the teacher explained the itinerary for the class, Wendy's attention and eyes drifted to a clear panel of glass above a dark green door which connected through to the classroom next door. She could see the antics that were going on. A man's bald head came into view through the glass panel and seemed to glide along as he held an orange tambourine high in his hands, shaking it. He must have been skidding past the door in his socks, Wendy realised, stifling laughter. Her nostrils flared as she tried to keep her amusement inside.

She raised her eyebrow in her "Wendy look" – as her mother would call it – skeptical and amused.

She could see a woman around the age of seventy who wore a bright yellow feather boa standing and hitting a tambourine again and again while shaking her large bottom. A man around the age of forty walked up to her with a pair of maracas and shook them as hard as he could, with a beaming smile. The skidding tambourine man soon joined them, rattling his tambourine with a wild grin.

Wendy turned her gaze back to her sign language partner, trying to keep a straight face.

"My doctor said that losing my hearing wasn't so bad – maybe this is what he was referring to," she signed to her partner, making the sentences with her hands, while mouthing the words too.

Her partner, a friendly lady in her fifties, began to laugh, and the teacher looked across at them sternly.

This was a quality that people who got to know Wendy admired. If they weren't too serious to understand her, they could see that, through her jokes, she had great resilience and a very upbeat attitude. Humour was her medicine.

She could take the dark days and depressing times that she had faced, and turn them into quick one liners and jokes – as if turning the world on its head and showing the world that *it* was the joke – and that she wouldn't be beaten.

It was a kind of rare sunshine that she would always find inside herself, a grit that kept her going in difficult times.

The teacher saw Wendy looking through the door and now marched over to it, pulling a roller blind down to mask the mayhem next door.

Wendy raised her eyes, turning to her partner. "It's funny," she signed. "Of all the classes a person could take, they paid for the one that lets them bash a tambourine like a five-year-old."

Her partner smiled, thinking about what Wendy had said. It took her a moment to formulate what she wanted to say using her hands.

"Maybe that's just life," she shrugged. "We never grow up."

Wendy nodded. She picked up her sign language book and flicked through it, looking for some words and gestures that she was slightly unsure of.

"I feel . . ." Wendy moved her right hand up her chest with her middle finger bent slightly inwards at the large knuckle to indicate feeling. She continued, mouthing each word as she spoke and signed, ". . . worried right now."

Her partner looked at her sympathetically, touching her right hand to her forehead with her fingers together and then moved her hand forward and down, with her thumb and little finger out and the rest of her fingers tucked in.

"Why?" she mouthed.

Wendy thought for a moment and looked inside her book.

"Because I have lost my cat." Wendy pinched her right thumb and index finger together while the other fingers stood up. Her fingers were shaped like a little teardrop and she moved them from in front of her mouth sideways. This was the sign for cat.

Her partner looked concerned. She was thinking of something useful or comforting to say to Wendy.

"Well, at least tomorrow is the weekend – you will have time to look for her," she signed, raising her eyebrows at the end hopefully.

Wendy froze in her seat. "What did you say?"

Her partner looked startled. She wasn't sure if Wendy had understood her signing correctly. "I said it's Friday. Tomorrow is the weekend," she signed again, this time very slowly and clearly. Her hands shook a little as she finished signing; Wendy seemed to stare through her and it was unnerving.

"Friday?" Wendy said loudly now while signing. She stood up in the middle of the classroom. "Friday?" she repeated, with a wild look on her face. "I've got to go!" she called, signing as fast as she could.

Without a word, Wendy grabbed her bag and ran from the classroom as the teacher called after her. She ran down the austere college corridor, its shiny laminate flooring reflecting the dull yellow lights above.

As she ran from the building, the mad sound of kazoos and triangles, tambourines and drums – all being bashed simultaneously by the silly adults in their "musical" class – seemed to follow her in an awful racket. Somehow, they summed up exactly how she was feeling.

CHAPTER 15

Mrs Budnick's Son

Wendy pulled up outside her house and switched off the engine. She leapt from her car, pressing the lock button as she ran to Mrs Budnick's front door.

It was Friday. How could she forget? She had been given a week to find the cat a home and now, the cat had disappeared. It couldn't be a coincidence.

Wendy's heart raced, and she knocked hard on Mrs Budnick's wooden front door. One. Two. She counted to herself, then knocked again, harder still. The little door rattled with each knock and Wendy held her knuckles with her other hand as they throbbed from the vigour of her hammering against the wood.

Finally, inside the house, a hall light flicked on, glowing warmly through the stained glass window above the door. Wendy could see the top of Mrs Budnick's curly hair approaching her from down the hallway. It grew closer, like a little cloud floating along, until the door opened a crack, then wider, as Mrs Budnick saw that it was Wendy standing there.

Mrs Budnick stood in the doorway wearing a floral apron. Her hands were covered with flour and she placed them upon her hips and smiled at Wendy.

"Wenditchka!" Mrs Budnick exclaimed and saw that Wendy's face was alarmed. "Whatever is the matter?"

Mrs Budnick looked at Wendy with concern. She pushed her glasses up onto her nose, leaving a dot of flour on the shiny purple frames.

"Hello, Mrs B!" She stared ahead for a second, thinking what to say. "I was just – do you have the cat?"

Wendy stared back at her, frozen to the spot. She was wide-eyed, her green coat wrapped tightly against her, her hair frizzy and untamed.

Being direct wasn't something that Wendy was very good at. But right now, she didn't care about etiquette or politeness. She needed to know exactly where the cat was.

Mrs Budnick eyed Wendy up and down and seemed to draw in a breath when she heard Wendy's question. Her old face grew very serious and she looked down her glasses at Wendy – it was a very stern look – as though she were an old judge in a grey wig and red robe at court. Wendy shook the image of Mrs Budnick in a court-room from her mind.

"I see," Mrs Budnick said as she clasped her flour-covered hands together with a little clap, and some of the flour rose up in a puff around her.

"You should . . . better for you to come in," she continued, beck-oning Wendy in with an open hand. "I thought this might happen," she muttered to herself, shaking her head.

Inside Mrs Budnick's living room, Wendy sat in an armchair. A round clock nearby with a gold interior and large Roman numerals beat out the seconds. It began to chime – an odd, slightly hollow sound emanated from it. Wendy's foot bounced up and down impatiently as she waited. She felt ready to explode. Finally, Mrs Budnick came into the living room carrying a tray with hot chocolate and some chocolate covered biscuits.

"I thought you would like this. You young ones always like the chocolate." She smiled, placing the chocolate biscuits beside Wendy.

Wendy smiled appreciatively, shifting impatiently in her chair. Mrs Budnick saw this. She could see that Wendy was bursting with questions and she knew only too well why.

"So tell me, Wenditchka." She handed Wendy a porcelain mug painted with roses. "Why you come for Cat? She not spend much time here, you know," she said with a wry smile and placed her own cocoa on the dining table beside her. Mrs Budnick sat down, facing Wendy, and let out a little sigh as she did. Her eyes looked wide behind her bifocal glasses as she looked at Wendy, waiting for her explanation.

Wendy wasn't sure where to begin in telling Mrs Budnick just how much the cat had influenced her life for the better. There was so much to say.

"Well," she began slowly, running a finger along the smooth side of her mug, "you see, I didn't think I wanted the cat in the beginning. But now –"

"Now you like Cat," Mrs Budnick interjected. Wendy nodded in absolute agreement.

"Yes, now I – I really like her. She has become, well . . . a friend. And I wondered if I could have her back to keep. She has been helping me out at home and then recently – and this is really beyond anything – she actually saved me from a –"

Just then Mrs Budnick's son, Olek, strode into the living room, cutting Wendy off as she spoke. He was about six foot three, with shining jet-black hair and was so sturdy that he looked like he could toss a cow as though it were a tennis ball.

"Ah, you hear about Cat." He shook his head at his mother. "Didn't I tell you? I said, 'Don't take it to them,'" he said in a strange, high voice, which was meant to be him quoting himself. "'She will want it,' I said – but you never listen to me."

Wendy nearly dropped her hot chocolate.

"What?" she exclaimed, placing the chocolate down with a clink, her eyes wide, her mouth open aghast.

Olek turned to Wendy and without any introduction ploughed into the conversation. "You talking about Cat, right?" He shook his head mournfully.

"Olek!" Mrs Budnick tried to interject.

"Yes, yes, I am," Wendy exclaimed, leaning forward in her chair. Her mouth went dry and she felt like her stomach had a giant elastic band around it, crunching it into a tiny little ball.

Mrs Budnick interjected again, waving a hand.

"No, I took it to –"

"She took it to man in white coat – he look like shock to see it," Olek interrupted, shrugging his shoulders casually.

Mrs Budnick pushed her glasses up on her nose, her cheeks reddening. "Excuse me, Olek, it was not 'man in white coat,' he is your –"

"I think it escape the needle once before, you know?" Olek interrupted again. He took a sip of his mother's cocoa from her mug on the dining room table. Mrs Budnick raised an eyebrow at Olek and he put the mug down.

Wendy looked at them both like they were insane. She wasn't sure what she had walked into. Was it possible that Mrs Budnick was really a heartless cat hater and not, in fact, a sweet old lady who loved cats? It wouldn't be the first time that Wendy felt she had been duped by someone appearing to be nice on the outside, when they were mean on the inside.

"No, that can't be right. What are you saying?" Wendy said, trying to remain calm. Mrs Budnick waved her hands at Wendy, shaking her head vigorously.

"No, no, it is not what he say!"

Wendy turned to Olek now, ignoring Mrs Budnick's plea. "When did she drop off the cat?"

"Yesterday." Olek thought for a second, enjoying the fact that Wendy was asking him questions now – and not his mother. "Yes, yesterday. Maybe, it make nice hat now." He started to laugh, a deep bassy laugh that seemed to rattle about the room.

"Olek!" Mrs Budnick stood up in frustration. She turned to Wendy. "I told you, Wendy – when Olek comes, Cat must go!"

Wendy didn't know what to say. She was just shaking her head in disbelief.

"But I don't understand. You took the cat away on Thursday! You said it would be Friday . . ." Wendy stopped mid-sentence. She couldn't believe what she was hearing. "I'm so sorry. This is all my fault!"

She wasn't apologising to Mrs Budnick, but to the cat – the cat that she held in her heart and mind. She looked down forlornly, trying to suppress the urge to cry. Olek shifted in his seat and raised an eyebrow at her.

"Ah, cheer up!" he said, shrugging his shoulders again. "You forget soon; there were many, many cats there. Maybe they find you new one – better one." He smiled, a wry cunning smile.

Wendy froze in her seat. She shot a searing look across at Olek, and her eyes narrowed dangerously.

"What do you mean?" she said sternly.

Mrs Budnick looked at Olek furiously. "Olek, stop it! This is not One-Oh-One Dalmatian. Nobody make any coat."

Mrs Budnick took off her glasses and placed them in her apron pocket. "Wendy, dear, I took her to the animal place. I am sorry."

Wendy looked confused and looked from Ms. Budnick to Olek, frowning. Olek smirked at Wendy; he had succeeded in winding her up so much that she didn't know what was happening anymore.

"The animal shelter?" Wendy said, now standing up from her chair. She hadn't touched her hot chocolate and it sat cooling on the table beside her. Olek saw it and reached over, picking it up. He began to drink it with a smile on his face.

"Yes, the animal shelter place. She will be absolut-e-ly fine. She is very safe there," Mrs Budnick confirmed, looking Wendy in the eye seriously.

"Oh my goodness! What time do they close?" Wendy exclaimed.

"I think it eight tonight." Mrs Budnick looked worriedly at the clock in her living room. "But they move Cat tomorrow. They said the place full, but a shelter in another town has space for Cat. I'm sorry Wendy, I did not know. Olek gets red skin when he near Cat, then he look like a wasp attack him. I thought I was doing good thing."

Wendy checked her watch; it was now seven thirty in the evening. She started to make a hasty exit, moving towards the living room door.

"Right. I have to go, I need to call someone . . . I need to find his number, he works at –"

Wendy didn't bother to finish her sentence; she was out of the door like a rocket, running as fast as she could back to her house.

"She'll know you are coming!" Mrs Budnick called after Wendy. "Ears like a hawk, that one!"

The front door slammed and Mrs Budnick and Olek were left alone in the living room. The clock ticked, filling the silence with each deliberate beat. Olek sipped on the hot chocolate that he had taken from Wendy, a satisfied smile on his face.

Mrs Budnick turned to Olek, snatching the chocolate away from him with a hand that moved so swiftly, it was like a cat grabbing a mouse.

"Idiot!" she exclaimed, before marching into the kitchen to continue with her baking.

CHAPTER 16

The Race is On

Frantically, Wendy rummaged through the contents of her office desk drawer, looking for Simon's phone number. She pulled out a ruler and a stapler and continued with a handful of sticky notes, pens and pencils. Exasperated, she pulled out the entire drawer and emptied it onto the desk in front of her. A roll of tape tumbled to the floor, and paper clips and staples scattered everywhere. But nowhere could she find the scrap of paper with Simon's number.

"Think, Wendy! Think!" she said. She tapped her chin with her fingers, scrunching her mouth to one side in anxious contemplation. Where could the piece of paper be?

"Ah-hah!" she cried, remembering her green coat – that was the one she had been wearing the day she met Simon. It was downstairs in the kitchen on the back of a chair. It must be in the pocket!

She flew down the stairs, almost slipping midway as she sped down towards the kitchen. She rounded the corner and skidded into the kitchen on the shiny floor tiles, sliding towards the dining table. She grabbed her coat from the back of a chair and shoved her hand into the pocket. Feeling around inside the pocket she felt a small piece of paper, and pulled it out hopefully. It was just a mint wrapper. Dejected, she put her hand back in and felt around more; she reasoned that it could be crumpled in a corner of the pocket. It wasn't there though – all she found was a loose mint and a receipt for some treats that she had bought for the cat. She looked at the receipt with a sigh. Still, she couldn't give up!

She turned to the coat's other pocket, her fingers feeling about everywhere, but there was no sign of a piece of paper, just an interesting white pebble that she had picked up somewhere a long time ago.

Now, there was only one pocket left; it was inside the jacket. She unzipped it fast and squeezed her hand into the small opening. She felt around. At first it seemed like there was nothing, but then her fingertip touched something, right at the bottom of the pocket. Crumpled into the corner of the pocket, something scratched against her fingertips – it was a piece of paper. She strained her fingers further into the pocket, reaching for it. She grasped it, pulling it from the pocket. She turned the crumpled piece of paper over in her hand and – her heart seemed to skip a beat – there it was: Simon's number – at last!

She pulled her phone from her pocket and dialed the number. The phone rang and rang. She waited, holding her breath, hoping that with each ring there would be his voice answering her call – that he could safeguard the cat for her and everything would be alright.

But there was no answer. Finally, her call went through to a mechanical sounding voice, which instructed her to leave a message "after the tone."

"Hi, this is Wendy," she said after the beep. She was exasperated. "I need your help. You see, I didn't want the cat, but now I *do* want the cat." She rambled, flustered. "She actually saved my life and although I may have started out against her, I actually see now that she – well – I just really need her and I would like to have her back – so please

call me!" The phone made a loud beeping sound, indicating that the voicemail had stopped recording.

Wendy put her phone back in her pocket, thinking. She needed to act fast. She ran to the hallway and picked up her purse, pulling her car keys from it.

Nobody was going to take the cat away from her now. She would go to the shelter and take the cat back herself.

Determined, she started up her little blue car. Its engine buzzed as it was brought to life, almost as though it were excited. Hastily, she pulled away from the curb, the tires squealing.

She accelerated fast now, tearing down the road. There was absolutely no time to spare. She didn't know who might take the cat or what might be happening to her.

She hurtled down small winding roads and decided to take a short cut that could easily shave ten minutes off her journey. It was a narrow, bumpy road that crossed a small stream – a ford. As she drove along the road, she came to the ford. It was near the end of the road, just before a larger road that would take her directly to the animal sanctuary Wendy stopped the car abruptly and cursed out loud.

"Oh, stinknation!" she cried. She had made up the word as a young child and now, in this time of strife, she yelled it into the night air.

In front of her, the ford was flowing high, as the spring rain had been abundant, filling the rivers and streams and flowing in from the nearby farmer's fields. The car's white lights illuminated the ford, and it flashed like liquid silver, snaking in a fast and deep torrent across the road. It made her heart skip a beat.

She was caught in a dilemma: if she turned back, she would never make it to the shelter in time and the cat would be moved to another shelter and, as to the location, she would have no idea where. How would she explain to them that this was her cat and that she had given it away by accident? She would certainly never see the cat again.

Her only chance was Simon – she needed to speak to him. He understood the situation and he could help her to get her cat back.

She took in a deep breath and revved the car's small engine. She began to drive through the torrent of rushing water. It circled around the car like a gaggle of boisterous imps, swirling and encircling the vehicle. It lapped against the sides of the car and came right up to the bottom of the doors. It bubbled and slapped against the car and the wind blew outside, making great old willow trees bend and twist eerily at the other side of the ford.

Wendy drove slowly, cautiously, not wanting to stall the car, not wanting to flood the engine. She could feel the stream begin to turn the car; quickly she tried to counter-steer, moving the wheel so that she stayed on course. The water was powerful and the wind seemed to grow stronger outside. Detached twigs from the nearby trees smacked at the windscreen. The car was being buffeted off-course by the wind, and she risked being swept downstream. Wendy accelerated a little more.

She pushed on through the rushing water, the other side looming closer. Finally, she felt the car rise up onto the slope at the other side of the road as she left the treacherous water behind and rejoined the muddy road at the other side.

The rushing ford lay behind her, babbling and scolding as it streamed across the road, daring drivers to cross it at their peril.

She looked to the clear road ahead of her. The stars were bright in the sky and she was now close to the shelter. She could do this; she knew it.

Wendy arrived at the shelter at ten minutes past eight and jumped from her car. Although it was past closing time, a light was still on inside the reception building and there was still one car parked outside.

She ran across the round paving stones to the reception building. As she grabbed the handle to the door; she felt her heart beating like a drum. The handle didn't budge. She shook the door handle vigorously and the glass door rattled in its frame. She could see that the office lights were on, so someone must be there – unless the lights were just on for security – she didn't know. But she was going to find out.

She banged on the glass and called out loudly.

"Hello!" She was stressed and her voice came out thin and high. "Hello!" she repeated again, shaking the door as hard as she could.

This time, someone came walking towards the door. She could see that it was the cheeky girl who had given her Simon's number. Her stomach sank a little – she knew that the girl wasn't going to be easy. She had seen the way she had behaved with Simon, teasing him and rolling her eyes.

Sally approached the door and waved at Wendy through the glass.

"Hi!" Wendy said, pointing to the door handle. "It's locked. I just need to ask you something – "

Sally smiled again, then turned her back and began to walk away.

"No!" Wendy cried, banging on the glass door.

Sally turned around laughing. She thought that it was funny to pretend that she was leaving. Wendy felt irate and Sally could see this, but she didn't seem to care. Sally walked back towards the door, taking her time and opened it, just a foot, peering out at Wendy as though she was a burglar.

"Hi," she said, raising an eyebrow suspiciously. "What do you want?"

"I've come to get my cat back." Wendy said without hesitation. Sally looked confused. "There was a mix-up," Wendy continued. "Someone brought my cat here and actually it was a mistake."

Sally sighed and rolled her eyes. "Right," she snorted, looking at Wendy dubiously. "Well, the shelter closed at eight, so I'm afraid I can't help you right now. But if you'd like to come back tomorrow, then I'm sure someone can speak to you about it." She made a false smile and started to close the door. Wendy quickly slid her foot into the doorframe, creating a wedge and making sure that Sally couldn't close the door on her.

"Please move your foot," Sally said, annoyed, as the door hit Wendy's shoe.

"Not until I get my cat back. I'm here now and it's not difficult. You must know where she is," Wendy said, adamant.

Sally rolled her eyes and shook her head, feigning exasperation. "It's not as simple as that."

"Well, tell me. Why isn't it? Please," Wendy said, adding the "please" as an afterthought. She really begrudged having to use the word with someone as petulant and rude as Sally. But right now, she was so close to the cat that she realised she had to try and keep her cool and be polite – even if she did want to charge past Sally and retrieve her cat.

Sally still had her hand on the door handle and Wendy still had her foot in the doorframe. Sally looked at Wendy; she could see she was stressed. If she had been truly mean, she would have enjoyed turning her away, but thankfully, she wasn't. She looked back towards the desk behind her, then back at Wendy.

"Oh, OK," she said, begrudgingly. "But this has to be quick. I can't stay here long, I've got plans."

111

"Thank you!" Wendy said, obviously relieved. Sally opened the door again and Wendy quickly followed her into the reception.

Sally walked behind the reception desk and pulled a large, red, cloth-bound book from behind the desk. Its pages were tatty and it looked quite old. It had a small red ribbon as a page marker that had become threaded and the pages were covered with fingerprints and dirt.

Sally noticed Wendy looking at the book and read her expression.

"We're moving over to computers this month – finally," she tutted. "We just keep this as backup while the system is being implemented."

"Oh, right," Wendy said, nodding her head, feigning interest.

"We were going to implement one a few years ago, but it just wasn't reliable and we didn't have the funding for tech support. That's what I heard anyway."

"That's, interesting." Wendy said, trying to sound upbeat – she really didn't care; she just wanted her cat back.

"It says here," Sally began, slumping the book on the table between them, "that your cat was adopted this afternoon. I wasn't in until five, so I don't know anything about it."

"What?" Wendy said, shock filling her face. She felt like someone had just thrown a bucket of icy water at her.

Sally looked petulant. "Well, I volunteer so I can't get here until five on Fridays." She made a defiant face, misunderstanding Wendy's shock.

"No," Wendy said, screwing up her face at Sally, unable to contain her annoyance. "My poor cat!"

"Oh, right, yeah." Sally nodded. "She was adopted," she said as she looked down at the book again, "at around four-thirty this afternoon."

"Does it say who it was?" Wendy strained to see over the counter and Sally pulled the book away from her.

"I'm afraid I can't give you that information, I'm afraid." Sally tried to sound official, but instead just sounded silly repeating herself. "I'm not even going to look – I really don't know who adopted the cat."

"Well, I'm afraid, I need to know who it is. That is my cat and you had no right to adopt her out, or give her away." Wendy was ready to go to battle for the cat.

Sally looked at Wendy witheringly.

"Hang on, hang on – just wait a second there – I thought you wanted to get rid of the cat! And now, here you are accusing, myself, of some kind of fraud." She touched her chest as if mortally wounded and tried to sound official again.

Wendy breathed in deeply and used her best "reasonable" tone: "No, I'd just like to know where she is so that I can contact the person who took her – and let her know that, actually, she has a home."

"Right, well, I can't do . . ." Sally's phone began to ring in her pocket and she stopped and looked at the screen. Wendy looked up to the ceiling, shaking her head. "Can you just hold on a second? I need to take this." Sally raised her index finger to Wendy as if silencing her in a continued attempt to be official and in charge. She noticed Wendy's eyes looking hungrily at the logbook and now slammed it shut, placing it back behind the reception desk. Then she turned on her heels and trotted through a door beside the reception desk.

"Hello." Wendy heard Sally answer her phone. "Oh Ian, yeah I know, yeah, I just finished."

Wendy listened for a moment and, as she did, she realised that she had two choices: she could stand there and wait for Sally to finish her call and be ushered away from the reception. Or, she could take matters into her own hands and see what the book said.

Quickly, she ran behind the reception desk, her heart pounding in her ears, and crouched down, pulling the large logbook from its shelf. She rested it on her knees as she crouched on the floor. It was heavy and musty and the pages seemed to go on forever.

She flicked through the yellowed pages, each one representing dozens of animals who had been in search of homes and finally found them. Page after page, they went on. The bookmark served no purpose – it was so shredded that parts of it sat inside multiple pages and none of them were the page she was looking for. She heard Sally's voice rise in the room beside her.

"Yeah, don't worry, I'll be there. I just have someone I have to get rid of. Yeah, I know it's way after closing – oh, don't I know it!" Sally exclaimed loudly as Wendy flipped frantically through the pages, her eyes flitting from the pages to the door beside her.

Wendy could hear that Sally's call was wrapping up now and her legs shook as she crouched, ready to spring away. Her fingers also shook and slipped on pages. She lost her place for a moment. Then she bit her lip and moved forward through the pages. Faster and faster she went, flicking through the pages. Finally, there it was. The afternoon entries for that day. About halfway down the page, written in small handwriting was the only description that made sense to her. It had to be the cat.

Small Tabby Cat .... S.B. ....
221 Pender Street, Apt 137, Sunnymede

Wendy grabbed a pen from the counter and began to scrawl the information across her hand.

"Two-twenty-one Pender, apartment one-thirty-seven," Wendy whispered to herself, repeating the information in her mind. Before she could finish writing everything down, Sally strode from the doorway.

"Hey!" she cried, her eyes wide, her hands in the air like jazz hands.

Wendy stood up from the floor like a jack-in-the-box, dropping the book. It hit the floor with a loud thud. For a split second, she felt like she was frozen to the ground, unable to move.

"I'm going to make you rub that off your hand – you can't do that! I'll call the police! I'll tell the police to go to the new owner and – intercept you – and . . ."

Before Sally had time to reach her, Wendy jumped up and slid over the shelter counter. Pens scattered everywhere and she nearly fell as one rolled under her foot. She ran frantically for the door. Sally chased her, snatching at the hood of Wendy's coat and screaming in a rage.

Wendy didn't remember opening the door. She didn't remember running across the carpark or getting into her car and starting the engine. But she *did* remember Sally. Sally chasing her. Sally yelling. Sally in the rear-view mirror, chasing the car. Sally jumping up and down, just a dark figure in the distance behind the car now – her fists shaking in the air, puppet-like in her movements – and then finally, as Wendy drove, Sally disappearing from sight.

CHAPTER 17

The Stranger's House

Wendy arrived outside the apartment building – this was the address that she had found in the log book. The building was fairly new and was surrounded by neat pathways and borders of shrubs. Moths flickered under a street lamp and a dog barked nearby.

She had stopped twice to ask for directions, driving around in circles and getting trapped in a loop on the town's notorious one-way driving system. But finally, she was here. This was the address in the sanctuary logbook.

She didn't know what type of person had adopted the cat, whether the person might be kind and understanding or might be indignant. She had imagined all kinds of people as she drove towards the mysterious Pender Street address. She had introduced herself about a hundred times in her mind.

"Hello, I'm Wendy. You have my cat." Somehow, she couldn't see that line working. She realised that she would just have to see what happened when she got there. She was so used to planning her future – planning around her hearing loss, waking up and imagining how it was going to be for her – that she realised now: *sometimes you just*

don't know until you get there. Take each day as it comes, because we can't know the future.

It was an unusual kind of realisation to have in the midst of such stress and worry.

She climbed a small iron staircase up to a brightly lit hallway and looked at the apartment numbers posted on a silver plaque on the wall.

Apartments 101 to 140 to the left and apartments 141 to 180 to the right. Large arrows pointed in either direction and Wendy took the arrow to the left, heading towards apartment 137. She followed different signs with arrows as she walked along a bright cream-coloured corridor and then followed another flight of stairs up towards another brightly lit corridor. This one had light blue walls.

After a few minutes of walking, she came to a reddish-brown wooden door with bronze numbers pinned to the top. It was apartment 137.

Wendy hesitated for a second, staring at the numbers on the door. She could feel her breathing getting faster. She felt hot and nervous. She raised her knuckles to the door. Then she paused, holding her breath, and stepped back. She felt a surge of adrenaline and stepped forward again quickly. She rapped her knuckles on the door and almost hopped on the spot in fear and anticipation and worry and excitement. She couldn't believe she was doing this. A complete stranger. She had followed the cat all this way and she was now at this apartment.

Oh, goodness, she thought, *I must be losing my mind. What am I doing? This is insane. What if they come at me with a frying pan . . . or a baseball bat?*

She thought she could hear someone coming closer to the door – and she felt the urge to run – but her feet stayed anchored to the spot. Next she heard a definite sound, a latch moving behind the door, and then it slowly opened. At first she couldn't see who it was. Then a light flicked on inside the apartment next to the door and a young man stood in the doorway in a blue t-shirt and jeans. He looked at Wendy with a surprise and Wendy took a step back.

It was Simon.

His look of surprise quickly turned into a broad smile and he raised his eyebrows as if to say "It's you!" He ruffled his hair with his hand subconsciously and straightened his t-shirt.

Wendy looked back at him, still grasping the situation.

"So . . . you . . ." She trailed off, not sure how to phrase everything she wanted to ask.

"I . . . live here?" Simon said, smiling at her. "Yes, I do."

Wendy nodded, thinking for a moment. "I'm sorry, I'm just a little confused." She pulled her coat around her, suddenly feeling cold. "Did you get my message?"

"Yes, actually, I just got it a moment ago!" Simon looked at Wendy as she held her coat closely to her. She looked tired. "Why don't you come in?" He opened the door wide and gestured with his hand, bowing slightly.

"You know," Wendy said, still standing in the same place, not yet accepting Simon's invitation to come inside, "today has been like some kind of murder mystery for me."

Simon raised his eyebrows again, this time amused. "I can imagine!" He smiled. "Well, why don't you come in, Miss Scarlett, and let me give you some clues!" he said, in a cheesy detective voice.

Finally, Wendy smiled. She laughed softly and walked into the apartment. Simon closed the door behind her and, facing the door, chastised himself for his silly detective voice. It was so cheesy – he wanted to act cool in front of her. Turning to face her now, he composed himself and offered her a seat.

"Can I get you something to drink?"

119

Wendy thought about asking him for tea, but it seemed too forward. "Just some water would be nice."

"Water it is." Simon smiled and turned towards the kitchen, then stopped and turned back. "I've also got some cookies if you're interested – double chocolate?" he said, enticingly.

Wendy loved chocolate and was happy to accept. "Go on then," she said, smiling.

Simon's apartment was small but interesting. He had a red sofa with a knitted shawl across it. The pattern on the shawl looked Northwestern or Native American. On the wall behind the sofa, a photo of a glistening lake stood out, dancing with sunlight. Next to the sofa there was a small table with an ostrich egg on it and a globe. It seemed that Simon had different travelling mementos and clearly liked to travel. Wendy's eyes darted as she looked around the room for the cat.

Simon quickly returned with a glass of water and a plate with two large chocolate cookies on it. He handed the plate to Wendy. She took the water and a cookie and bit into it, enjoying its rich chocolatey taste.

"Not bad?" he said, smiling, watching her take a large bite from her cookie.

"They're delicious!" she exclaimed.

Simon smiled. "I baked them. It's my aunt's recipe. Two things she loves: cats and baking."

"She sounds like a lovely lady," Wendy said, smiling. Simon smiled back. He was happy to see her.

"I'm sorry to just charge over here like this," Wendy continued, "but I was hoping that – speaking of cats – you might have my cat?"

"Ah yes." Simon said. "Well, I don't have *your* cat, I'm afraid."

Wendy stopped eating her cookie.

"What?" she questioned. A crumb was stuck to the corner of her mouth and her face looked crestfallen.

Simon cleared his throat anxiously. "Actually . . ."

Before Simon could continue, the cat stepped into the room and saw Wendy. As soon as it saw her face, the cat came scampering joyfully across the room, its little furry legs moving in a blur. The little cat rubbed her soft cheeks against Wendy's shin and she knelt down, kissing the cat's head lovingly. Wendy pressed her head gently against the cat's silky-soft head and then picked her up, holding her like a little furry baby, and looked into the cat's beautiful green eyes.

Wendy shot Simon a look.

"I don't have *your* cat – I have *your grandmother's* cat!" he said, grinning.

Wendy gently reached over, so as not to disturb the cat – and promptly shoved Simon from where he was sitting. He laughed and fell backwards, spilling water down his t-shirt as he tumbled from the large beanbag that he had been perched on.

"What?" Simon questioned, jokingly, his hair all ruffled from his tumble.

"Anyway, how did you get my address? I was going to text it to you when I received your message and then you appeared, here! I suppose Sally gave it to you."

Wendy gulped and tried to suppress a smile. "In a manner of speaking."

Simon looked at her with wide eyes, still smiling. "What did you do?" he said, disbelievingly.

Wendy shook her head at him, smiling. "I'm sure you'll hear all about it on Monday." Simon shook his head and laughed. "I can hardly wait," he said as he rolled his eyes. He looked fondly at Wendy and the cat – they made a very sweet picture.

Wendy looked down at the little cat, softly cradled in her arms. The cat's big green eyes looked up at her, shining love out towards her from a deep well within. Wendy felt very lucky. She gently tickled the cat's pretty head, and the little cat bristled her white whiskers, moving her pink nose close to Wendy's face, as if kissing her. Wendy kissed her on the head again and held her close.

Simon looked at them both, smiling; his eyes were kind and soft. He moved closer and petted the cat, looking up at Wendy.

"Beautiful," he said, looking at Wendy.

Wendy looked back at Simon and blushed slightly. She knew that he meant her. She shifted and changed the subject.

"So, has she been eating?" She cleared her throat, self-consciously. "Has she been exploring the apartment?"

"Oh yes, she's very much the explorer." Simon shook his head to himself, as if about to say something, but then stopped.

"What, what is it?" Wendy asked, curious.

"Oh, well, it's just, she's very unusual."

"Unusual?" Wendy said, raising an eyebrow. She hoped that this wasn't about the news – maybe Simon had been watching the TV and had seen the news report about the cat who had stopped the burglar – and had figured out that it was *her* cat! *No, that's crazy thinking,* she told herself and shook the idea from her mind.

Simon saw Wendy's anxious expression. "Oh, it's nothing." He stopped talking, and then changed his mind again. "Actually it's not – would you do me a favour?"

"Sure," Wendy said, a little uncertain. "As long as it's not anything weird," she joked.

Simon laughed. "It's not weird."

"OK, well, go on then." Wendy was very curious now.

"Can you just go outside and ring the doorbell or knock on the door. I'll close the door – and then when you come to the door, I just want to test something out."

Wendy had clued in now. It was the cat. He had seen her at work. Her powers as a hearing cat – hearing and sensing all of the different sounds within the house and helping out where she could.

"Oh, OK," Wendy said knowingly. She smiled and gently put the cat down on the carpet, stroking her silky fur as she did.

"Don't worry," she told the cat as she looked up at Wendy, baffled. "I'll be just outside the door. I'm coming right back in." The cat looked up and winked her eyes at Wendy.

Simon scratched his head thinking. "Hmm, maybe, walk down the corridor a little bit if you would, and then wait a minute or two before walking back."

Wendy laughed. "Sure."

She did as Simon had asked. She actually waited five minutes and walked some distance away from the apartment around a curving corridor. Then she slowly walked back, taking gentle quiet steps, and rang the doorbell to Simon's apartment.

Simon had gone into his small office space and was sitting at his desk in front of his computer, listening to some music with headphones on. He never heard the doorbell and so stayed seated at his desk.

All of a sudden, the cat came running towards him at full speed and jumped onto the desk in front of him, tapping his arm with her paw. She looked at him very seriously, her pupils large and dark in her big green eyes.

Once he was paying attention to her, she dashed towards the front door and Simon followed her, opening the door to Wendy.

"Tah-daah!" Simon exclaimed as he opened the door and the cat stepped out, winding her silky body around Wendy's legs.

Wendy grinned broadly. "She told you I was here, didn't she?"

"She certainly did!" Simon said, clapping his hands together in excitement.

"I now realise she's a trained hearing cat," Wendy said, scooping the little cat up in her arms. Wendy stepped back inside, seating herself on the red sofa and wrapping the beautiful blanket from the sofa around herself and the cat. The cat looked just like a little furry cherub in her arms, bundled up in the soft blanket.

Simon looked at them both. It was delightful.

"I'm just wondering," Simon began as he settled himself into his beanbag and continued munching on his large chocolate cookie, "why you would need a cat that can hear things. I mean, she would be amazing for someone who actually needs . . ."

"It's hereditary," Wendy blurted out. This was the one question that she had been dreading all along. She didn't mean to just blurt it out – it was private and yet, part of her just wanted to be done with the inevitable, to move on from it, like pulling a plaster from a wound as fast as she could.

"Oh, I see," Simon said, nodding his head. He was a little slow; he looked quizzically at Wendy. "You mean . . . hearing loss is hereditary in your family?"

Wendy felt like covering her head with the blanket. She felt her face growing hot and her throat tightening. Wendy really liked Simon – he seemed interesting and fun – and now she felt he was going to reject her. She had come to expect it from people who didn't know how to relate to her. She *didn't want* to be treated differently – why couldn't people understand that?

All this suddenly caused her anxieties and pain to come welling up, a cascade of everything that had been building within her – the way she felt rejected by the medical system and by callous people in society – situations where people make unfair judgments of those who are different. Some of these people she had actually met; others she had never met; and some she felt she would have to encounter in the future. She felt them all ganging up in a wall inside her mind, conspiring against her, judging her, calling her names.

Simon realised that he had been heavy-handed and quickly tried to make amends.

"Wendy, it doesn't matter," he said gently.

"It does matter. It really matters," she said, and she felt like crying. "She was my grandmother's cat and my grandmother lost her hearing, but that was later in life than what's starting to happen to me. I think . . . I think she must have trained the cat and I never knew." She shook her head and a hot tear rolled down her cheek.

"I never knew. I didn't fully appreciate what Grandma went through, or how she lived – or the cat, when she was in her home." She sighed heavily.

Simon looked back at her with empathy on his face. He wanted to hug her.

Wendy continued, taking in a deep breath. "I never paid attention to the cat because my parents are obsessed with them, in a way that isn't normal – and I . . . I always resented them. My grandma was always so cheerful and she could lip read and . . . it never seemed like she couldn't hear. She was like sunshine."

She didn't know why she was being so open about everything. Her emotions were just rolling out of her now, like waves on the ocean coming to shore. Normally, she would have made her excuses and been out of there in a flash. But, there was something about Simon's manner that allowed her to open up. He was genuine.

Simon looked at her, his brows furrowed in empathy.

"She's purring," he said, nodding to the cat in Wendy's arms. He wasn't changing the subject, but he wanted Wendy to be aware that she had a friend in her arms who was there for her.

Wendy looked down at the cat. A tear rolled down her cheek and she caught it before it splashed onto the cat's fur.

"She belongs with you. She's purring," he said again. "You can feel her love. The vibration of her purr."

Wendy smiled at Simon now, wiping her face with her hand. He was right; she could feel the cat's love, not just in the ways that she cared for Wendy, but also in the vibration of her purr. She didn't need to hear it, to feel it.

Simon looked back at Wendy and a thought occurred to him. His eyes seemed to light up as they sparkled with an idea.

"If you don't mind," he said tentatively, "I've got something that I would like to share with you that I think can express better than I can, what I want to say."

"Oh?" Wendy said, sitting up now. She wiped her tears from her cheeks and looked at Simon's sparkling eyes. She was genuinely curious. He seemed full of energy suddenly.

"Yes, you said your grandmother was like sunshine; like it was stored inside her." He smiled. "I think you have that sunshine too," he said, looking at Wendy sincerely.

Wendy looked down, trying to hide the smile on her lips.

"Come on, let me show you," he said, standing. He offered Wendy a hand, but she didn't take it. She didn't need to be helped. She felt more aware of her pride, especially after opening up her emotions to Simon, and didn't want to be treated like a "maiden" as she called it. It was just the way she was.

"Let's see what you think," Simon said as he turned and walked across the living room. Wendy paused, looking at the cat in her arms for agreement. The cat looked back, her green eyes winking gently.

"OK," Wendy agreed, nodding at the cat.

She followed Simon to his study room, padding across the soft carpet with the cat in her arms and the red blanket draped around them. Simon stood in the doorway, opening the door wider for Wendy and the cat. Wendy stepped through the door. Upon entering the room, the first thing in view was a typical home office: a computer, some paper, and a few note pads. Simon nodded, gesturing to the far wall further inside the room. Obscured behind the door was a large and very beautiful painting. It was wondrous – a hidden gem.

Different shades of blue seemed to stream from the canvas, a strip of brilliant green. Silver leaf dashed across the canvas with a smattering of white, like forks of light blazing on water.

Simon turned to Wendy. "I painted this a few months ago during the winter."

"It's beautiful," Wendy said, clearly impressed. "You're very talented."

"Thank you." Simon leant forward and touched the painting. "I wanted it to be more than a painting. I really worked at building the texture so that it is three dimensional." He looked at Wendy and nodded his head encouragingly. "Go on," he repeated, "you can touch the painting – please."

Wendy raised an eyebrow. "It's amazing. But I don't understand why you . . ."

"Just try it, go on," Simon interjected, keenly.

Wendy shrugged and obliged: she leant forward, touching the painting with her fingers. She ran her fingers slowly across the dense paint.

"Now close your eyes," Simon said earnestly, encouraging her.

"What?" Wendy exclaimed. She thought this was a bit strange.

"Go on, close them. Seriously, I'm not going to be weird," he said, laughing.

Wendy looked at the cat again. She looked calm. Gently, she put her down on the floor.

"Well, she seems calm, so I'll give it a go," she said, looking down at the cat. The cat sat between them now, looking at the painting too.

Wendy began to touch the painting with her eyes closed, with both hands she traced the lines of the paint, ebbing and flowing across the canvas. Parts were high like jagged mountains, then low and smooth like valleys. It felt cool to the touch and somehow calming.

"Now open your eyes." Simon said gently.

Wendy opened her eyes and the painting and lamp-lit room came back into view. She felt better now. Somehow the intense feelings that had coursed through her felt as though they had drifted away somewhere.

"What do you imagine when you feel the painting?"

Wendy contemplated for a moment before answering. "A cool ocean, I think."

Simon nodded his head, visualizing this.

Wendy continued, closing her eyes again. "Voices carried on the breeze. The sweet smell of coconut sun cream. Eating pineapple. The waves on the shore, the sound they make as they arrive."

Simon smiled. "And you could hear that with your eyes closed in a silent room." Simon turned to face Wendy now. "You're more than the sum of your parts, Wendy. Anyone can see that."

Wendy looked back at Simon, a half smile across her lips. What he had said was truly touching.

"Thank you," she replied after a moment.

"Your imagination and memory can take you anywhere you want to go. You will never be without sound when you can remember and create. No one and nothing can take that away from you."

Wendy looked at Simon with great warmth. She leant down and picked up the cat again, kissing her head fondly.

"Well, I certainly have a second pair of ears here too," she said, smiling at the cat.

Simon petted the cat gently on the head. "She's quite something." He looked at Wendy again. "Would you like anything else to eat or drink? I feel like I should be a better host."

This was his way of hoping that he could get her to stay a little longer.

"Oh, thank you," she said, but she was weary now. "I would, but it's getting late and I need to get her home," she said, rocking the cat in her arms.

They walked towards the front door together and Simon picked up the wicker basket from beside the door.

"I don't think we'll be needing that," Wendy said, nodding at the cat basket. She looked to the cat for agreement and the cat wiggled slightly in her arms. "No, I think she's decided that she doesn't need anything as archaic as a cat basket. She said it's like a corset for cats – restraining and silly."

Simon laughed: "Sounds about right." He wrapped the red shawl that Wendy had picked up from the sofa more tightly around her and the cat to help keep them warm. "You can keep this." Wendy smiled, touched by his kind thoughtfulness.

He opened his front door and Wendy walked out, smiling. She turned and looked at him.

"Thank you – for everything." She smiled. "We won't ever forget it." She paused in the doorway, looking at him.

This was his chance, he realised. He had to seize it. If he let her walk away now without saying anything, he wouldn't forgive himself.

"How about dinner tomorrow – maybe at six?" he blurted out. This time, he was the one blushing.

Wendy looked at him for a moment longer and then nodded, smiling. Her eyes were bright and shone like sapphires.

"Six is good." With that, she turned and walked down the corridor, carrying the cat in her arms. Simon watched her walk away, her auburn hair swaying at her shoulders.

He couldn't see, but Wendy was grinning from ear to ear as she walked.

"What an evening," she whispered to the cat, unable to keep the smile from her face.

CHAPTER 18

Sounds Like Love

Wendy sat at the white vanity table in her bedroom, brushing her hair. She wore a deep red dress; she looked beautiful. She put on the pearl bracelet that her grandmother used to wear and her lipstick was a deep red. Her blue eyes shone and her auburn hair lay curled at her shoulders.

The little cat sat on the floor beside her, watching her apply the finishing touches. She wore a red velvet collar which stood out against her pretty tabby coat and she looked very dignified.

"I don't know about you, but I think you look good in red," Wendy said to the cat, tickling her head. The cat looked back, winking at her.

"I have decided we have to re-name you. I'm going to call you Hawkie. Ears of a hawk, you have!" she said, smiling at the cat.

Wendy stood up and straightened her dress, checking her reflection in the long mirror beside her bed. Turning to look at Hawkie, she smiled a radiant, happy smile.

"I love you," she signed to Hawkie, emphatically crossing both hands over her heart and pointing to Hawkie.

The cat looked up at her and bristled her whiskers as if saying "I love you too!" Wendy lowered her face to the cat and she snuffled her little pink nose at Wendy, as though kissing her.

Then Hawkie turned and promptly walked to the bedroom door.

"Charming!" Wendy raised her hands, questioning Hawkie. "Oh, you want me to follow you?" She placed her hands on her hips, raising an eyebrow at Hawkie.

The little cat looked back at her, as she stood poised in the doorway, one paw raised for action.

"No surprises, please; I don't think I can take any more!" Wendy said, slipping into her red heels.

With that, Hawkie leapt through the doorway, and bounded down the staircase. Wendy shook her head, her hands on her hips, and rolled her eyes.

"What now?" she breathed to herself.

Carefully, she made her way in her red dress down the stairs and rounded the corner into the hallway. She looked down the hallway and could see that Hawkie was sitting on the doormat and staring up at the front door impatiently, her neck almost straining, her head up vertically, gazing at the door handle.

"OK, OK!" Wendy said, shaking her head. "Keep your fur on!" she said, giggling at her own joke.

As Wendy approached the door, Hawkie leapt up and pulled down determinedly on the door handle. Wendy's eyes widened with surprise. She laughed; she was delighted and impressed. *Yet another skill,* she thought.

Hawkie almost succeeded in opening the door but, ever since the repair from the burglary, the door needed a bit more of a pull. Wendy pulled the door further in, opening it slowly. Hawkie impatiently crammed her furry head into the gap between the door and its frame and then, before the door was even fully open, she slipped through the gap, as though she were made from rubber.

"Be careful!" Wendy exclaimed. But Hawkie didn't care. She was off, trotting towards the front gate and out onto the street. As Wendy stepped out of her house, she looked down to see a brown box on her doorstep.

"How strange," she said to herself, picking up the box. She looked up to see Hawkie waiting at the gate impatiently, as if to say, *Well, hurry up then – open it, I'm waiting.* Wendy smiled at Hawkie and began to pull the box open. As she opened the first flap of the box, shining blue paint was revealed and a stout pair of legs; it was Mr Nettles! Wendy pulled the box open completely, grinning as she did. Grandma's gnome stared up at her with his beaming smile.

"Mr Nettles!" Wendy exclaimed, laughing. Her parents must have left him there for a joke. She shook her head, still laughing, and placed Mr Nettles beside her front door before closing it.

"OK, I'm ready!" she told Hawkie, catching up with her at the gate. Hawkie bristled her whiskers in a little smile and slipped through the gate, eager to continue with her plans. Wendy followed Hawkie as she trotted along the street and was forced to jog to keep up.

"What is it now?" she called out to Hawkie, who was always two steps in front of her.

The little cat scampered through Mrs Budnick's front gate and towards her front door, her black-tipped tail flicking and waving as she trotted.

Wendy followed her, then raised her hands in questioning as the cat came to a halt – right at Mrs Budnick's doorstep!

"I know it's Mrs Budnick's birthday, Hawkie – we were just about to come here next – if you had given me two seconds!"

Wendy raised her hand to knock on the door and, before she could even touch it, the door suddenly opened. Wendy jumped like a cricket, pulling her hand back quickly as someone stepped out. Mrs Budnick's front door was like a cuckoo clock!

It was Simon! He let out a small yelp, not expecting anyone to be standing that close to the door.

"Wendy!" Simon exclaimed as he stepped back.

"Simon!" Wendy cried.

"It's you!" he replied, flustered. He carried a bouquet of flowers in one hand and in his shirt pocket, the nose of a brown toy mouse with wiry whiskers was poking out. It looked very funny.

"How are you?" Wendy said, still gathering herself. "What are you doing here?"

Simon looked back at her and Hawkie, smiling now. "Well . . . I could ask you two the same question! I'm at a birthday party, as it happens."

"Oh, we are too!" Wendy exclaimed. "Yes, it's Mrs Budnick's birthday – what lovely flowers you've brought for her, she'll be thrilled, I'm sure." She pointed to the beautiful flowers in Simon's hand.

"Actually, these are for you." Simon handed Wendy the flowers, to her happy surprise. It was a beautiful bunch of flowers, pink and white peonies with a large red rose at the center. She looked down at the flowers and smelled the rose.

"They're absolutely beautiful." She smiled, breathing in the rose's delicate scent.

"Hmm, I know the feeling," Simon said, looking at Wendy in her red dress, a cheeky grin on his face.

Wendy raised an eyebrow at him, grinning. "Um, I think you're forgetting someone." She gestured to Hawkie beside her.

"Oh, a red collar!" Simon noticed Hawkie's new collar and smiled. "Well, excuse me for being so brash. I need to make sure I compliment all the beautiful ladies here today!" he said, grinning at Wendy.

"That's better," she teased him.

He opened the front door wide now, gesturing for them to come in. "Speaking of beautiful ladies – please, come into the party!"

"Thank you", Wendy said as Hawkie ran through the door ahead of her.

"Just so you know – I have dinner booked for us at seven – I don't want you to get too carried away with the game of charades they're playing in the back garden!"

Wendy giggled at this; she could imagine Mrs Budnick would be a formidable player.

135

Simon bent down and tickled Hawkie's head where she stood beside him. "I was just on my way over to see you – I was going to come a little early and invite you to the party. It's so cool that you live right next to my aunt."

"Your aunt?" Wendy exclaimed with surprise as they walked into the living room.

Simon stood beside the dining table where an array of biscuits and cakes sat.

"Yes," he said nonchalantly, as he picked up a butter cookie and began to munch on it. "Before we go and join everyone in the garden you should try my aunt's baking – it's amazing!"

On the table, behind the cookies, there were framed photos of Mrs Budnick from throughout her life. There was even one of her as a little girl with flaxen hair. It was a celebration of her life in photos.

Simon saw Wendy looking at the array of photos. "That was my idea. It's nice, isn't it?"

"Yes," Wendy said, distantly. "So, Mrs Budnick is your aunt," she continued, piecing things together in her mind, "and you're the nephew – you must be the one who likes animals?"

Simon laughed. "Yes, that would be me." He crinkled his nose, embarrassed. "So she's been telling you about me – it's funny, isn't it? You live so close to each other."

Wendy nodded. "Sure is." Then she thought about it. "Well, now it's funny, I suppose. I mean, really, it's more funny peculiar than funny ha-ha."

"Funny peculiar." Simon laughed. "I like that."

Wendy shook her head as if dazed. "I just can't believe she's your aunt. It's incredible really, I mean she . . ."

Just then, Hawkie shot up from the floor and onto the dining table, knocking a large silver frame from the back of the table. The frame clattered onto the ground, stopping Wendy in her tracks.

"Hawkie!" Wendy cried. "What are you doing?" She picked up Hawkie and put her back down on the floor.

"Sorry," she said to Simon, tucking her hair behind her ear. "I don't know what got into her."

"Oh, it's fine." Simon said, picking up the silver frame and standing it back upright with the other photos. "What were you saying?"

Wendy glanced at the frame and noticed the photo inside. She did a double take. She grabbed the frame and held it close to her chest – her eyes were like saucers.

"I can't believe it!" she cried, her eyes and mouth wide as she stared at the photo.

"What?" Simon exclaimed, seriously worried.

"Mrs Budnick," she began, now staring from Simon to Hawkie. "She's your aunt."

"Yes, Wendy," Simon confirmed again, looking very confused.

Wendy turned the photo to face Simon. "This is my grandmother." She pointed to the photo emphatically. "I see now that your aunt and my grandmother were friends."

In the photo, Mrs Budnick and Wendy's grandmother sat side by side, pressing glasses together. It was summer and they were both wearing floral t-shirts. They were both a lot younger and it looked like an era from many years ago. The car behind them was a strange brown colour, like milk chocolate, and they both wore their hair curly and long. Wendy guessed it to be sometime in the Seventies.

"Wait, hang on," Simon said. Now *he* was the one who was wide-eyed. "That's her old friend – Gloria."

"Yes, my grandmother – Gloria!" Wendy affirmed.

Simon shook his head in disbelief. "She was telling me about her just the other day." He stopped, still processing the revelation. "My aunt said she was sad it had taken her so long to move back from Ukraine and that Gloria had recently passed away... she had wanted to visit her."

Wendy looked at the photo sadly and handed it to Simon. He held the photo, looking at it with a new sense of understanding.

"They had been writing to one another and, when she didn't get a reply recently, she worried that perhaps something had happened to Gloria."

Wendy nodded, her eyes sad.

"She told me that she had called the house, but there had been no answer. Then she saw in the local newspaper an article about Gloria – your grandmother – passing and it really broke her heart."

Wendy's eyes began to fill. "Sorry," she said, as a tear rolled down her cheek. "I never knew. I had no idea they had been friends. If I had known, I would have comforted her."

Simon took the frame, placed it back on the table at the center, and turned to Wendy. "Don't apologise," he said, wiping a tear from Wendy's cheek. "Well, the same goes for you. Had my aunt known, she would have comforted you too." He gave Wendy a big hug. "She will be thrilled to learn you're Gloria's granddaughter." Wendy, Simon and Hawkie all faced the photo now, looking at it with stunned awe.

They stood together, hugging in the living room and Hawkie looked up at them both.

"Ouch," Wendy said, moving away from Simon.

"What?" Simon looked down at his shirt pocket. "Oh right," he said, laughing. He realised that he still had the mouse in his shirt pocket and Wendy laughed too.

He pulled it from his shirt and presented it to Hawkie.

"This, Madame, is for you," he said and gave a flamboyant bow. Then he crouched down beside Hawkie and gently tickled her head as she raised her pretty face up towards him happily and placed her paw on the mouse. Wendy crouched down beside them both.

She shook her head, thinking to herself. "You know what's even funnier than your aunt and my grandmother being friends? The fact that Hawkie had never even met your aunt, yet ended up being drawn to her."

"Yes," Simon said, nodding. "You're absolutely right! My aunt was back in Ukraine when your grandmother got Hawkie. Auntie never even met Hawkie."

They both looked at Hawkie now as she gazed at them, her eyes glistening with a kind of magic.

Wendy laughed a joyful laugh and sighed. She raised her open palms to the sky in a shrug of acceptance.

Wendy looked from Hawkie to Simon and smiled lovingly at them both. Hawkie gazed back at her, her new toy mouse at her feet, and Simon looked at Wendy with his bright, kind eyes.

Wendy placed her hand upon Hawkie's soft fur, gently stroking her silken coat. She felt Hawkie's delightful purr vibrating through her fingertips. A soft, tranquil energy seemed to radiate from her; she could indeed feel her love.

A purr can tell a thousand stories, Wendy thought as Hawkie's purr vibrated joyously through her fingertips, like a divine Morse code. *Its greatest message – love.*

Wendy looked at Simon, her hand softly resting on Hawkie. The clever tabby cat happily purred and purred, her beautiful furry face soft with contentment.

"Sounds like love," Wendy said, looking at them both.

CPSIA information can be obtained
at www.ICGtesting.com
Printed in the USA
LVHW070053020821
694284LV00004B/4

9 781525 592980